BETTIE PRIVATE INVESTIGATOR SHORT STORY COLLECTION VOLUME 3

CONNOR WHITELEY

No part of this book may be reproduced in any form or by any electronic or mechanical means. Including information storage, and retrieval systems, without written permission from the author except for the use of brief quotations in a book review.

This book is NOT legal, professional, medical, financial or any type of official advice.

Any questions about the book, rights licensing, or to contact the author, please email connorwhiteley@connorwhiteley.net

Copyright © 2023 CONNOR WHITELEY

All rights reserved.

DEDICATION

Thank you to all my readers without you I couldn't do what I love.

AUTHOR OF THE ENGLISH BETTIE PRIVATE EYE SERIES

CONNOR WHITELEY

CRIMINAL PERFORMANCE

A BETTIE PRIVATE EYE MYSTERY SHORT STORY

CRIMINAL PERFORMANCE
20th August 2022
Canterbury, England

Private Eye Bettie English had seen some stunning performances at various theatres all over the United Kingdom. She had seen the breath-taking opera in London, amazing comedies that made her stomach hurt for days on end afterwards in Edinburgh and she had seen the sweetest little production done by children for the various charities that she gave money too.

But this performance was just criminally bad.

Bettie sat on a very comfortable little red seat in the circle of the Bluebird Theatre in Canterbury, this was probably the best seat she had ever had because its delightful softness, a black cup holder in the arm that was actually large enough to hold her diet coke and the seat was dead-centre in line with the middle of the stage.

The large(ish) black stage itself wasn't exactly

grand, it was probably nothing more than some wooden blocks stuck together to give a very convincing look alike to trick people into believing it was a professional stage, but Bettie just knew better.

The smell of sweat, peanuts and amazingly rich bitter coffee filled the air, and Bettie was so looking forward to next month when she gave birth to her twins and she could finally have some of the delightful black gold again. She had really missed her coffee.

The roar below in the stalls came from tens upon tens of proud parents shouting, laughing and pretending to enjoy the performance going on the stage. Bettie wasn't sure if they were actually faking it or pretending or Bettie certainly was.

Currently on the stage were a group of 3 to 4-year-old toddlers with a pop song on in the background, and from what Bettie could understand the toddlers were meant to be dancing judging by the adult dressed in black moving around trying to encourage the toddlers to do the same.

But come on, they were toddlers. Bettie had absolutely no expectation that they were going to dance, sing or whatever.

Bettie just smiled as she heard her wonderful boyfriend Graham next to her huff. Clearly he was just as sad about the lack of performance as she was, he was probably just too kind to say anything.

Then next to the other side was Bettie's sister Phryne in her little black dress cheering, shouting and clapping at the little toddlers. Bettie wasn't exactly impressed that her sister had basically tricked her into coming along to this performance for the charity she gave her time too.

Bettie had never ever known her sister to be charitable in the slightest, hell this was the exact same sister who didn't really seem interested that her son, Sean, and his boyfriend, Harry, were living with Bettie, rather than his own mother after they were attacked and Harry had a brain injury.

"Now everyone please clap your hands together for the amazing, the stunning, the spectacular Thomas High Schools Girls," someone said over the microphone.

Thankfully the little toddlers who looked so scared and concerned hurried off, even though one didn't understand what was going on so she was walking towards the edge of the rather high up stage. An adult grabbed her and they all left.

A few moments later some 5 to 6 years olds (Bettie had no idea how they were classed as high school girls) came onto the stage dressed in rather… inappropriate clothing for that age (or any age really).

Bettie rested her hands on her baby bump. "Please tell me you two aren't going to be into this show stuff,"

Bettie almost jerked at the baby kicks and Bettie just smiled at her two beautiful babies. She firmly took that as a no, and she more than loved them for it. Of course if the twins had wanted to do this then she would have let them.

But she preferred them not to, for now anyway.

"Miss Bettie English?" a woman said in the darkness.

It took Bettie a few moments to realise that there was a middle-aged woman dressed in all black standing right next to her. It was so dark in the theatre Bettie was struggling to see her own baby bump let alone someone dressed in all black.

"Yes," Bettie said, still not being able to see the woman clearly.

"Are you the Private Eye woman?" she asked.

Bettie rolled her eyes at the sheer dismissiveness that the woman said it with.

"I am,"

"Great," the woman said and leant closer to Bettie. "We need your help please. There is a situation that we cannot call the police about. Can you please help us? My boss has authorised the transfer of a thousand pounds as compensation,"

Normally Bettie would have at least pretended to consider not taking the job because of course she was with the family she loved, watching a cute little child performance and supporting a charity she loved.

Absolutely none of that was true in the slightest.

Bettie grabbed the woman's hand and shook it hard. She was going to take any old excuse to get out of here.

She quickly told beautiful Graham was she was

doing and he just stuck his tongue out at her in jealousy. Bettie didn't blame him but at least she was escaping.

But the theatre wanted to give her a thousand pounds. That was a lot of money for a few hours of work.

Bettie was more concerned about the case than she ever wanted to admit.

***

A few minutes later the middle-aged woman, which admittedly had seen better days with her oversized body that was putting such a strain on her black uniform that Bettie was waiting for the buttons to explode off, led Bettie into a bright white storage room that was a bit on the small size for a very overweight woman and a heavily pregnant woman to get into to.

Bettie really wasn't a fan of its bright white walls, musty smell of sweat and Bettie even saw a very well-used condom on the floor so she could only imagine what this room was actually used for.

Yet what really caught Bettie's attention was the makeshift desk covered in papers and the grey metal filing cabinet that had been forced open.

"This is the problem Miss English," the middle-aged woman said, pointing to the forced open filing cabinet.

As much as Bettie wanted to focus on the filing cabinet she was a lot more interested in all the papers on the desk. It was strange how the criminal or thief or whatever had gone to the filing cabinet when there was clearly so much paperwork on the desk.

"What happened?" Bettie said as she looked through the paperwork on the desk.

"This is my storage room and office," the woman said. "And my name is Miss Savannah Claire. Before every performance I exit my office, lock it before I go and meet the production crew to double check everything is ready,"

Bettie nodded as she was reading the bank account information and passwords on the desk. It was stupid that the theatre would leave their bloody banking passwords in the open, but she wasn't their investor or anything to do with them.

It was still stupid.

"I leave my office at half 1 and I checked with the production crew. Then I watched the opening performance of the show at two. I just had to leave after that," Savannah said.

Bettie couldn't exactly blame her too much. If she had been smarter Bettie would have realised then that the pointless opening of the performance with a mixture of toddlers, who didn't know what to do and were too nervous because of the crowds, and older children, looked more like a chaotic cat fight more than a so-called elegant performance.

"Then I came back to my office and found the filing cabinet open,"

Bettie could only nod as she found another cold

piece of paper that detailed out the theatre's business plan, taxes and employee passwords. This was beyond stupid now and it was a wonder that the theatre hadn't been robbed before.

But why leave this information and not take it?

Bettie looked at Savannah and folded her arms. "What was stolen?"

Savannah looked to the ground. "Someone stole the scripts of a brand new West End performance coming down from London. This performance would have put the theatre on the national and international map,"

Bettie wasn't sure about that but if a little theatre like this could host such a massive performance that would have had positive reviews, be critically-acclaimed and have some great stars then it would definitely be a boon to the theatre.

And most importantly the person who worked in there.

Bettie quickly realised that this theft wasn't about money or anything like that, it was about sabotaging the livelihoods of the people that worked here.

Bettie picked up the recent bank documents off the desk and reread them, and the theatre was cash-strapped up to their necks. They had maxed out all their credit cards and the theatre probably had two months left at best.

"Can you help us?" Savannah asked.

Bettie didn't react and just went over to the filing

cabinet had stunk of strawberry lube, sweat and a very strange earthy aftershave that Bettie hadn't smelt in a long time. She had bought it for Graham years ago before they broke up and he had hated it. He actually had an allergic reaction so bad Bettie had to take him to hospital.

Besides from that the filing cabinet (well that draw that had been forced open anyway) was perfectly clear. Then Bettie focused on the two marks where something had been forced into the draw to pop it open. It looked like a simple crowbar job but that was a little too simple for Bettie's liking.

"Do you keep crowbars in the theatre?" Bettie asked.

Savannah nodded and pointed under the desk.

Bettie rolled her eyes as she popped her head under the makeshift desk and saw an entire toolkit. She didn't want to know why Savannah had all of these tools but she guessed Savannah was also a part-time handywoman too.

This place was really cash strapped.

Bettie folded her arms again. She had some scripts stolen, no evidence in the filing cabinet, the breaking into the filing cabinet was done with Savannah's tools so that proved nothing and there were no clues in this storage room.

Bettie was at a dead end.

"Is it possible for people to get into the theatre during a performance?" Bettie asked.

Savannah looked a little annoyed at even the

suggestion.

"Of course not. That is ridiculous. The theatre has had thefts before but I will not allow them anymore. I make sure this place is secure,"

Bettie actually believed her and at least the dead end meant she was going to be working a little longer so she didn't have to go back to the god-awful performance.

But Bettie did have a critical lead now.

If no one could get in it had to be an inside job. And that made Bettie even more curious about who it could be.

Was it one of the proud parents watching their kids in the stalls or was it a staff member?

Bettie was really looking forward to finding out.

***

The sheer dirtiness of the little box-room that apparently served as the security office only told Bettie more and more about how dire the situation was for the theatre. The security room was caked in dirt and dust and smelt like some teens had had a pizza party without bothering to clean it up.

Bettie really tried to focus on the little computer screen in front of Savannah as she showed Bettie the security footage. Bettie was going to do this bit herself but there was no chance in hell she was going to sit down in this room. And much less touch the wooden desk with the computer on, Bettie could see the grease covering the surface.

Bettie was actually starting to wonder if the theatre closing down might be a benefit to the local area. It would be at least from a public health perspective.

"This is the security camera outside my office," Savannah said.

Bettie was surprised Savannah thought these cameras would be useful. There was such a thick layer of ugly dust and grim on the camera lens that Bettie could hardly see the office door, let alone any details of the thin figures (presumably people) walking past.

This was another dead end.

Bettie was really not impressed now. It was almost like Savannah had purposefully kept the theatre in such a bad condition that it was useless to investigate if any crimes occurred.

Maybe that was the play.

"Bring up all employees in today please," Bettie said.

Savannah nodded and typed away at her computer a little. She bought up the employment records and Bettie was right about Savannah doing a lot of different jobs. She was the manager, handywoman and occasional extra if a play needed it.

Bettie admired this woman's resilience and lust to throw herself into everything that the theatre required of her. But Bettie also knew that this was where people tended to go to the criminal side of humanity out of annoyance, spite or another reason altogether.

"Where's the scripts Savannah?" Bettie asked.

Savannah huffed. "I respect you too much Miss to lie to you. You didn't know it but you were the first person in a long, long time to at least talk to me like I'm a person. And not some superhuman,"

Bettie had no idea she spoke to Savannah in a special way. She was just doing what she always did.

"How long have you been a one-woman band?" Bettie asked.

Savannah didn't seem like she could look at Bettie. At least she probably felt bad for her actions.

"Ever since last Christmas I have had to reduce staff levels by a factor of ten. I'm been repairing, fixing and cleaning believe it or not every day,"

Bettie found the cleaning comment hard to believe but to interrupt would just seem rude.

"I've been doing sixteen hour shifts every day this year. Finding stupid performances to put on, not paying myself living wage and it is just so trying,"

Bettie folded her arms. "What do the owners say? Have you told them?"

Savannah glared at Bettie. "You think I want this sixteen hours stuff. I don't. I really don't. My bosses tell me if I don't comply I'll be fired. I'll be on the streets. They own my apartment,"

Bettie gently placed her hands on her baby bump. This case was never what it had seemed in the first place, this wasn't a strictly criminal act, it was a call for help.

And Bettie actually wanted to help this poor

woman.

She needed to get the cops involved. She needed Graham.

***

A few hours later, Bettie and Savannah leant against the wonderful warm brick wall of a shop on the delightfully perfect cobblestone high street of Canterbury as they watched Graham escort a middle-aged man and woman down the high street towards his police car with two uniformed officers closely behind him.

Other people, as they strolled up and down the high street on this wonderful evening, muttered and looked and spoke about what was going on. Bettie laughed at some of the guesses like drugs, murder or kidnapping.

But the truth was a lot, lot sadder.

As a Private Eye and doing a lot of charity work too, Bettie had always known about modern slavery but this was the first time she had ever encountered it and it was the last time she ever wanted to.

Despite the sensational buttery, creamy, sweetest scents coming from the various bakeries on the high street, Bettie felt so sorry for Savannah. A woman who had been kicked out by her husband because she refused to put up with his drinking and shouting anymore. A woman who had been on the streets for months before two people offered her a way to freedom. A woman who had been tricked into believing enslavement was a freedom.

As Savannah watched with cold distant eyes at Graham walking away her captors, Bettie focused on her. For the past year and a bit, her captors had forced her to live in a tiny little apartment on an awful wage in awful conditions. They controlled everything about her life but because Savannah loved the theatre so much she didn't notice until it was far too late.

Then the scripts for the best-selling sensational West End performance came down to the theatre.

Bettie fully understood why Savannah had taken the chance and stole the scripts. Her plan was logical, hide the manuscripts away until the theatre was forced to close and then Savannah was going to sell the scripts anomalously back to the West End production company.

And hopefully (and Bettie admitted this was a massive gamble) the production company would still want to host the play at the Bluebird Theatre which Savannah would buy with the money from the script sale.

It was perfect.

Which was why Bettie had instructed Savannah to put the scripts back into the filing cabinet and pretend they were never stolen. So whatever was said Savannah wasn't a criminal and the focus was purely on the captors and the charges of modern slavery.

"What will happen to me now?" Savannah asked as she forced herself to look away from the police.

Bettie gently rubbed her baby bump as the twins

kicked in excitement.

Bettie was about to say something when her sister Phryne came over and hugged Savannah. Bettie was pleased that Phryne looked so happy considering Bettie had left her precious little performance.

"Savannah it is great to welcome you to the team," Phryne said.

Savannah's eyes widened. Bettie had no clue if it was out of fear or joy.

"The team?" Savannah asked.

Bettie gestured Phryne to explain.

"Of course my dear," Phryne said. "You are now the proud owner of the theatre. A certain detective made them sign it over to you before they were arrested and now our great charities get to work together,"

Savannah slowly nodded then Phryne wrapped her very thin arm around Savannah's chunkier one and started dragging her down the high street towards a restaurant for dinner.

Savannah looked at Bettie like a plea for help and Bettie just laughed. It was nice to see her sister get so excited about something for a change. It was actually nice that after all the chaos of late her sister was doing good, and she was even involved in a charity now.

As a delightful breeze of warm air enveloped Bettie, she smiled to herself and started to walk down the street towards where Graham went with the captors. She had no doubt the uniformed cops would take them back to the station to be booked and

Graham had the car keys.

So Bettie needed to be quick otherwise she'll be stranded in the middle of Canterbury, definitely not a bad place to be stranded but Bettie just wanted to go home now and enjoy her wonderful boyfriend.

Bettie kept walking, the rough cobblestone under her feet, and she couldn't believe how great she felt about today. She had helped a theatre survive, saved a woman from enslavement and even given her a brand new start as the owner of a theatre.

If that wasn't a great day's work, then Bettie really wasn't sure she wanted to know what was.

BETTIE PRIVATE INVESTIGATOR SHORT STORY
COLLECTION VOLUME 3

JUBLIEE, TERROR, CELEBRATIONS
2nd June 2022
London, England

Private Eye Bettie English had never really been too much of a royalist, but as a British person she had always kept an eye on the royal family, what they were up to and listened to Private Eyes when they spoke about secrets they had uncovered in their own investigations.

Bettie walked along a very long London street with little terrace houses lining the street with not a single parked car on the road and everything had been freshly polished and cleaned for this very special occasion.

With Bettie's boyfriend Detective Graham Adams being called in to help protect, control the crowd and provide security for the Queen's Platinum jubilee. Bettie was more than interested in wandering around London and then hoping to go up to the Mall, see tons of amazing people from throughout the commonwealth and hopefully watch the Trooping of the Colours as the platinum jubilee weekend officially started.

Bettie couldn't deny how excited she was that the Queen had been reining for 70 years and she had done a great job. Given the Queen had no political power, or not much power whatsoever, she was more of a cultural icon in this day and year, but Bettie didn't have a problem with it.

And that was probably why people loved, respected and treasured her so much. Because she had no power and she was part of the country's somewhat questionable history in the days of the Empire, people were always interested in how she had kept up with the ever-changing world.

Bettie had actually met the Queen once.

Bettie listened to the distant talking, shouting and other excited noises as thousands upon thousands of people gathered in London just hoping to see the Queen, the Trooping of the Colours and any members of the royal family.

It had been a few years ago when Bettie, some other Private Eyes and the current President of The British Private Eye Federation David Osborne had travelled to Buckingham palace to get an audience with the Queen.

And even though Bettie had expected and known she was a very kind, polite and down to earth person. She was still rather shocked by how much attention, respect and love that the Queen gave all of them.

Bettie would never forget how the Queen actually wanted to hear how Bettie found being a woman in this modern era and doing a so-called man's job.

Bettie loved the beaming hot sun on her face and her pregnant body as she wandered further down the long London street towards the sound of the excited tourists.

There was such a buzz of excitement, joy and celebration that captured all of London, and Bettie just loved it. It really was amazing how much London seemed to be alive today and united in the celebration of the Queen.

Bettie loved the wonderful smell of bacon, eggs and bitter coffee (that her pregnant body hated her to have) coming from a local café. And even though she started to feel ever so slightly sick at the smell of bacon (her body seriously didn't like animal products since she got pregnant) it was still a wonderful smell to start off today.

With Graham busy helping to police the crowds for the next few days, Bettie wasn't sure what she was going to do. Everyone had the next four days off so everyone could join in the celebrations.

So Bettie was more than looking forward to the wonderful street party that was going to happen on her road on Sunday. It would be simply wonderful seeing all her family and neighbours and friends coming together and celebrating together.

But Bettie was really just looking forward to the vegan food, the company and the non-alcoholic drinks. It might have been a time for celebrations but she was definitely not putting her unborn twins at risk.

The sound of two deep voices a lot closer than the excited crowds hundreds of metres away made Bettie focus on the long street. She had been the only person here a moment ago.

Then at the very, very end of the street were two very tall stone buildings, that there probably offices, there were a group of five men dressed in all black and they were quietly talking almost themselves.

The men were such a strange contrast to Bettie in her stunning flowery summer dress that hide her baby bump very well, her wonderfully comfortable high heels and her little black purse that only contained her phone and a credit card.

Considering the entire city was alive with excitement, affection and jubilation about this weekend, Bettie couldn't help but feel like this was something important.

Sure she knew that not everyone liked the Queen and the royal family. But even those people tended to at least acknowledge this was something to be happy about and they wouldn't dress in all black on a boiling hot day.

In the rare event that these men were going to cause trouble Bettie tried to figure out what the point of their meeting was at the end of the street would be.

Bettie noticed that the buildings were definitely tall enough to overlook the rows upon rows of houses and other London apartments in front of it. And if these men went to the very top of the buildings then they would have great line of sight.

If these people weren't dressed in all black then Bettie couldn't have cared about their great line of sight to the Mall, the Palace and other important roads involved in the Trooping of the Colours.

And in actual fact with the Queen's mobility issues in recent months (still amazing for a 96 year old), this was the only day the Palace had absolutely confirmed the Queen would be in London.

Bettie wanted to gasp and she felt her stomach tighten at the realisation that someone wanted to try and kill the Queen. Then this was definitely the day to do it.

Perhaps the only day.

Then the five men dressed in all black looked around, didn't see Bettie and they all went inside the taller one of the two buildings. Granted one of the buildings was only a metre or two taller than the other, but Bettie knew that was still important to snipers or whatever these people were.

The smart thing to do might have been to phone Graham, her handful of contacts from MI5 from a previous case or just called the police. But they wouldn't believe her.

Bettie knew from conversations with other

Private Eyes that there had been a dramatic increase in terrorist (both abroad and domestic) chat in the weeks coming up to the Jubilee celebrations. And with the war going on in Ukraine, Bettie knew that Russia was also plotting to destroy the Jubilee.

So MI5 and the police would definitely have their hands full without her suspicions, and because Graham's protection assignment was classified (Bettie only knew he was in London) she couldn't contact him.

Bettie was alone in this.

Just in case this was a terrorist attack and MI5 did want to listen to her, she sent a quick message to Agent Daniels, an agent she had met on a previous case, and just hoped that he would read the message.

But if that didn't happen Bettie wasn't going to let some idiots kill the Queen, spoil her weekend and become remembered in the history books.

No terrorists deserved that honour.

Bettie quickened her pace.

She was going to go into that very tall building.

And find out what the hell was going on.

***

One of the benefits of being a private eye was definitely that Bettie made contacts with all sorts of knowledge. Including a very serious security fault in most electronic locks installed by the *Mrs Locks* company.

Thankfully the very tall building Bettie had

wanted to get access into was locked as tight as Fort Knots but it had a Mrs Locks security system installed. So Bettie simply typed in *1, 2, 3* and the door opened for her.

Bettie went into a rather small black reception area with nothing more than a black desk, two black chairs and a lift door.

Bettie hated the musty smell that radiated from the chairs and it was rather clear that no one had loved this reception area for ages. But Bettie couldn't help but feel like the reception area was nothing more than a front for something.

The entire space just felt off for some reason.

Considering the building was so tall and massive from the outside, Bettie was surprised that it felt so small on the inside.

And even above the lift doors it showed the lift moving up the floors and apparently it had stopped on the sixth floor. But when Bettie placed her hand on the cold lift doors, she could feel that the lift was still moving upwards.

So why did the building or owners only want people to believe there were six floors?

Bettie noticed there were four security cameras in each corner of the reception area, so she went round behind the desk to see a very small computer screen build into the desk.

Bettie flicked through the security cameras. She couldn't even see herself standing in the reception area and apparently the lift was empty.

Someone had looped the feeds.

The door clicked.

Bettie just smiled to herself and she instantly knew that she was now locked in the building with five potential terrorists, so she definitely had a choice to make.

She couldn't break the computer screen and just hope that the building had professionally monitored security that wasn't being hacked, or she could try to unhack or unloop the security cameras herself.

Not that she actually knew how to do that in the slightest.

And it wasn't like she could call her wonderful nephew Sean and his boyfriend Harry (the computer experts of the family) because they were revising for some exams next week.

Bettie felt her twins kick inside her and she just knew that she had to press on, and try and find these potential terrorists herself.

Bettie turned her attention back to the computer screen and swiped away from the security cameras and she bought up a floor plan of the building.

As she expected there were apparently only six tiny floors in the entire building, but at least the floor plans were stupid enough to indicate the wall behind the reception area was false.

In fact there was even something about it being privately monitored and not on the main system, so if Bettie opened the wall. It would certainly alert someone.

Bettie turned and tapped the large black wall and it was certainly hollow.

Bettie couldn't believe how excited she was getting, so she looked back at the desk, saw a pair of scissors and she stabbed them into the wall.

A slight vibrating sound filled the air then fell silent.

Bettie quickly cut through the wall that was made with nothing more than very good-looking cardboard and she was very surprised to see a small dusty staircase in front of her.

This would definitely be the perfect way to sneak up the floors and past the potential terrorists.

The terrorists would probably be able to hear or feel the lift moving up after them, but the stairs would be perfectly silent.

Bettie was very glad that she could finally take off these damn high heels that might be comfortable but they were most certainly not practical for Private Eye work.

She gently kicked them off and placed them firmly at the bottom of the staircase so in case someone came in they would instantly know something was wrong.

Bettie loved the feeling of excitement grow inside her.

She raced up the staircase.

***

Bettie couldn't believe how outrageously hot it

was in the little pitch black staircase. She was so hot sweat was refusing to pour off her anymore.

She had been walking or stumbling more like up the stairs for twenty minutes until her hands felt a little wall in front of her.

The stairs felt awfully musty and dusty and just awful. Bettie didn't want to be in here any longer than she had to be.

"Snipers are activated," a man with a deep voice said.

Bettie was surprised that the man sounded so close even though he was on the other side of the wall. Bettie used her hands to search the wall in front of her and she was delighted to find some kind of switch.

She flicked it.

The entire wall collapsed.

Bettie gasped as all the five men dressed in black just stared at her.

Bettie had been expecting there to be a little secret hole in the wall so she could peek through them.

Clearly that wasn't what that switch was designed for.

Bettie frowned as five guns were fixed on her.

But Bettie didn't care. She was much more focused on the very tall muscular man in the middle, the only man not covering his face, holding two military issue guns at her head.

"Military. Former soldiers," Bettie said looking each of the men up and down.

Bettie pointed to the man at the other end of the little penthouse room she was in with thick glass windows all around them and no furniture. This had to be the top floor.

"I'm guessing snipers?" Bettie asked, as she watched the man expertly cut the glass so he could have a clear shot from the window.

Bettie gestured if she could get closer and the man holding two guns nodded.

Bettie just gave the former soldiers a quick nod of respect when she noticed that the sniper was staring at the balcony at Buckingham palace where the Queen would be standing in a matter of...

The distant sound of people screaming in excitement and the royal bands playing loudly and the clopping of horses made Bettie want to be sick. The Trooping of the Colours was happening now.

The Queen would be out at the balcony at any moment.

"Why this building?" Bettie asked. "And why am I not dead?"

The man with two guns just gestured to Bettie's baby bump. That was a massive relief.

"My other question?" Bettie asked.

"Eagle when the traitor is on the balcony kill her. That is my command," the man said.

"Confirmed," the sniper said.

Then Bettie was surprised to see the other three

men lowered their guns, walked behind Bettie and picked up a sniper rifle each.

With all the wall collapsing and the guns focused on Bettie, she must have forgotten to properly scan her surroundings. Then the other three men cut expertly done holes out of the class and aimed at the balcony too.

They were killing tons of the royal family.

"The building," Bettie said firmly.

The man with the two guns that was clearly the leader smiled and shook his head.

"You know what your Queen's grandfather did to our people," he said.

Bettie almost missed it but she was… she was a little surprised to hear faint hints of a Russian accent, but it was so faint that the men clearly hadn't been in Russia for decades.

In fact the men sounded so British and acted exactly like other members of the British Army Bettie had met before.

"Coming onto the balcony now," one of the snipers said.

Bettie noticed a red dot on the leader's ears and Bettie didn't know how she knew, but she just knew that she had to buy a little more time for something.

"Don't shoot yet. Don't you want the attack to be famous? Wait a few more minutes so the entire family is on the balcony, all the TV cameras and people are watching. Come on guys, this is basic!"

Bettie shouted.

"Hold fire for 60 seconds," the leader said.

Bettie didn't dare let her smile show.

Bettie walked straight up to the leader. "The building and what did the Queen's grandfather do to Russia?"

The leader huffed. "Your King George the fifth could have saved Russia and the royal family. You could have save Nicholas the 2nd, he could have allowed him to come to England. But he didn't. The entire family died, even the children!"

Bettie wasn't exactly sure what to say. She had studied the first world war and the politics and history of the three grandchildren of Queen Victoria and how they waged war against each other, but what could killing the Queen do after over a century?

Again she only needed to buy time.

"What could this killing achieve…"

Then Bettie instantly realised that the Queen was never going to be the intended victim, there would be the Queen's elderly adult children, her grandchildren and her great-grandchildren on that balcony.

And what better way to make the granddaughter of King George the 5th suffer than watching her own children die. Just like Nicholas the 2nd of Russia would have to do all before he died himself.

"This wouldn't change anything for Russia. This is only…" Bettie said.

The leader held up two guns to Bettie.

"This isn't about Russia. Russia can die. This is

about the British Royal Family learning what it means to suffer," he said.

There was no changing his mind.

Bettie took a few steps back and waved her hands.

Five bullets fired.

Five corpses smashed onto the ground.

Bettie's twins kicked in excitement in her stomach. She was seriously starting to wonder how much of a handful these two were going to be in a few months.

"Bet!" Graham shouted.

Bettie felt her entire body go weak when she heard her beautiful sexy Graham was coming for her. Granted he was a bit late, but better late than never.

Graham dressed in his blue Demin shorts, white shirt and black sunglasses and looked stunned as he walked up the stairs and looked at the five corpses in front of her.

"I always knew you could look after yourself," Graham said, kissing Bettie.

Bettie just nodded.

Then she smiled. She couldn't actually think of a better way to start off the Jubilee celebrations than by saving the Queen and the rest of the Royal Family.

As Bettie and Graham were about to walk back down the stairs (Bettie didn't want to be in a lift on such a hot day, not that the stairs weren't much cooler), she just looked at the corpses a final time knowing that the bodies would never be discovered.

"Long live the Queen," Bettie muttered as her and Graham went back down the stairs.

Then Bettie quickly told Graham the so-called reasoning for the attack.

"Makes sense in a strange extremist way. What better way to embarrass the royal family than on this historical occasion,"

Bettie nodded in the pitch darkness as she carefully went down the stairs.

"How did you find me?" Bettie asked.

Graham laughed. "Agent Daniels called. And I was already in the area dealing with some protesters but Daniels wanted me to ask you, do you know about the purpose of this building?"

Bettie smiled a little. She knew there was something wrong with this building in the first place, and it was even stranger than the police hadn't secured it. They had secured all the buildings that gave snipers a perfect shot of the Queen.

So why had they missed this one?

"I cannot say I do. Why?"

Graham stopped on the pitch black staircase.

"I think this was always meant to be a trap, a lure if you will for terrorists and I think this is some kind of government research facilities," Graham said.

As crazy as it sounded, Bettie completely agreed with him. This building was rather perfect in a way because it was tall enough for people to keep a look out for anyone about to invade the building, giving the government time to move their operations, and Bettie was sure the glass wasn't easy to cut into from the outside, and it would most certainly explain why the glass was so thick on the top floor.

It was so thick because Bettie wanted to bet it was bulletproof.

It had to be considering how dangerous it was for the snipers to poke their rifles out of the windows. Police officers, agents and everyone would be looking out for that sort of behaviour.

A very risky move for those terrorists.

Bettie and Graham kept walking down the stairs, and when Bettie went into the reception area she didn't even bother to pick up her high-heels again. She simply went straight out the door and back into the delightfully warm London air.

The air wasn't too hot and it was filled with the sounds of excited people and hints of sausages, eggs and bacon and it was filled with such a buzz that Bettie really felt alive.

And she couldn't be happier than she had helped to protect this amazing historical occasion.

Graham wrapped his amazingly strong sexy arms round her, and he started to kiss her neck.

"I am a plain clothes officer today. Want to help me?" Graham asked.

Bettie just smiled and pure excitement shot through her. She couldn't think of a better way to spend the day. She got to protect people, be with the man she loved and she got to celebrate with the country she loved.

And that was a perfect beginning to a perfect long weekend to Bettie.

DANGER OF OPEN WINDOWS
15th August 2022
Canterbury, England

Two months after the attack, Sean felt the anxiety afflicted him and stirred up in striking waves that seemed to smash into him for a moment before passing. He felt like the ground and the entire world would collapse around him, his chest might even explode and he was completely alone for those moments. Until the anxiety passed and everything returned back to normal. It wasn't really a way to live but at least the therapy was helping.

Sean leant against the warm wooden doorframe of his and his boyfriend Harry's bedroom with Harry an almost dangerously thin line under the thin blue silk sheets in their double bed, surrounded by some fine wooden chests of drawers, wardrobes and there was even a wooden black chest at the bottom of the bed.

Yet the roaring of Harry's snorting still managed to vibrate the spotlight-like lights in the corners of the bedroom, but Sean was just glad for any sounds coming from him. Because they all meant that the love of his life was alive, and that was all that mattered to Sean.

Sean never really did understand why his Auntie Bettie English, a private eye, had gifted them so much stuff when him and Harry moved in to help them recover after the homophobic attack. He partly supposed that it was because she felt guilty for some stupid reason, it was never her fault and it was her that had put the bastards behind bars forever.

Something rustled downstairs but Sean ignored it. It was probably just the neighbour cat after some of Bettie's tuna again.

If anything, it should be Sean's own mother and father who should feel guilty for what they didn't do. Even after Sean's mother's meltdown a few weeks ago where she confessed that she never wanted children so early anyway, Sean had wanted them to fix their issues.

But they hadn't.

Sean actually didn't mind that too much as bad as it sounded, he loved his Auntie Bettie and it was great to help out around the massive and expensive house as Bettie and her boyfriend Graham, a cop, prepared for the arrival of their twins.

The only problem with Harry being so tired after coming back from brain therapy was that it just meant he slept alone. Sean wasn't exactly a massive fan of that, because it meant him and Harry didn't have too much time for talking, making love and catching up on their days.

Yet considering that the first six months of brain therapy was the most important in making sure that Harry made a complete recovery, it was always far better to sacrifice these months with him now, than possibly lose him forever. Not that it really mattered anyway, considering Sean would love Harry no less.

"House is empty mate," someone said.

Sean froze and just focused on the thin line that was Harry under the sheets. Someone was clearly in the house, they were probably in the kitchen and making their way towards him.

Sean couldn't have them in here, what if they were going to beat him again? What if these people would finish the job of killing him and Harry? What if...

One... two... three...

Sean forced himself to take slow breaths until he counted to ten and he needed to focus. Bettie and Graham wouldn't be back for hours yet because they were in London at some big fundraising event for a charity. It was just Sean and Harry here for a while, and Sean couldn't risk waking Harry because he had another day of therapy tomorrow so he couldn't be tired for that.

Sean was alone, he had to protect his soulmate and he wasn't going to let some criminal idiots dare defile his Auntie's house.

Sean took out his smartphone and quickly texted Bettie that people were in the house. The smart thing might have been to call the police, but considering it was two police cops that had beaten him and caused Harry's brain damage. That was a last resort.

"Mate look at these pictures. That woman might be old but she's banging. Wanna wait for her to come home," someone said.

Sean's hands formed fists. How dare they talk about his auntie like that.

Sean forced his gaze away from Harry and turned to focus on the very long bright wooden hallway with the long wooden staircase with an iron railing down at the end. There was nothing in the other rooms that shot off from the hallway that would help him.

The only thing that could help Sean now was to confront the criminals and get them to leave.

Sean carefully tipped-toed down the hallway, making sure to focus on the top of the staircase in case one of the criminals was coming up. He couldn't get caught just yet.

He couldn't entirely understand how the criminals had gotten in, granted he had left the kitchen window open because it was too hot and he had cooked himself a chicken curry, so he hated to get rid of the smell.

But surely two criminals couldn't climb in through a window?

Sean reached the top of the staircase and normally its smooth wooden features looked so stylish, calm and great. But today Sean wasn't pleased with them, they made the house look too luxurious and like the perfect target for criminals.

Sean slowly started to go down the stairs. All he needed to do was reach the bottom of the stairs and look round the right-hand corner into the living room to see what was going on.

"Mate what you wanna do if there's someone here. We got a lot of stuff to search and steal," someone said.

Now he was closer, Sean knew that the *mate* speaker (the only one he had heard so far) was definitely a young male.

"We make sure they don't tell on others. Boss wants us to make sure this bitch knows not to mess with us," a slightly older female voice said.

Sean's heart started to pound. What if they were killers? What if they were dirty cops? What if they were going to beat him so badly he was brain damaged too?

Sean's world started to spin. This couldn't be happening again. He couldn't survive another piece of trauma. Not now, not ever.

These people were going to finish him off.

Sean felt the entire house move around him like it was going to smash down on him. Killing him.

One… two… three…

This was absolutely ridiculous and Sean was going to end this now. He was not having some idiots scare his Auntie, rob her house and endanger the man he loved.

That wasn't happening.

"Well, well, well," a young woman said from the bottom of the stairs.

Damn it. This is why he hated himself and his anxiety and those stupid cops. That had made him into this incapable idiot that was useless when he was alone, and not next to his amazing Auntie.

But Sean wasn't stupid.

He didn't speak, he only focused on the young woman in front of him and most importantly how to overpower her, all whilst keeping a good few metres from her and the small pocket knife she was carrying.

She definitely wasn't the prettiest of young women with her deadly black eyes and horribly dirty blue jeans and t-shirt. She didn't look happy to be here but Sean had seen the coldness in her eyes plenty of times before.

She hated him. And he hated her.

"Get up," the young woman said.

Sean didn't react or move. She wasn't in control here and most people would focus on the small knife at this time but Bettie had made sure to teach Sean why that was always a bad idea. Focus on the person so he knew what she looked like for a description later on.

And the knife wouldn't be the first sign of trouble. It would always be the idiot holding in.

"Get up now," the young woman said.

Sean slowly nodded and he almost liked hearing the sheer amount of annoyance, rage and anger in her voice. Whoever this woman was she never wanted Sean to be here.

Sean went down the stairs and hooked a right into Bettie's beautiful living room, and normally the massive TV hanging on the white walls, the cream-coloured three-seater sofa and two armchairs centred around a brown coffee table were normally so bright and loving and comforting.

But the mere presence of the strangers seemed to make the entire room seem sadder, lonelier with a slight shade of anger. That was properly what Sean was feeling, but he was just determined to get these young idiots out of the house.

"Yo mate?" a young man said from the opposite side of the living room as he came in from the kitchen carrying real silverware.

Sean had to admit the young man was rather hot considering he was wearing tight black jeans, a loose-fitting t-shirt that highlighted how muscular he was behind it and he had longish black hair.

But now Sean had both of the idiot criminals in his sights he just knew that he had to focus and make sure both of them were captured.

"Sit," the young woman said.

Sean smiled. "I'm not a dog. What do you two want?"

Sean was a little disturbed that the young man was just staring in utter confusion at him. It was probably something to do with Sean's blond hair with stylish streaks of pink running through it, but he didn't care what this criminal scum thought of his hair. He was going to have them both suffer.

Sean felt the icy coldness of the point of a blade jab into his shoulder.

"I said sit," the young woman said. "Then I will tell you exactly what we are doing and how you are going to help us,"

Sean highly doubted that but the criminals were willing to talk so he carefully sat down on the sofa making sure to keep both of them in sight.

The young woman sat on the coffee table.

"We are here because our boss wants your auntie to leave her alone," the young woman said.

Sean was impressed that she knew he was her nephew, but given how Bettie wasn't only a private eye but the President of the British Private Investigator Federation, it was only strange that someone hired these two.

It couldn't be related to a case because Bettie had only been doing background checks constantly for the past few weeks because she was due to give birth next month.

Sean seriously doubted it was anything to do with

the Federation because Bettie had been so focused on rebuilding it after all the corruption and whatnots of the last president.

"And breaking in will help you how?" Sean asked.

The young woman asked. "Our boss can get anywhere. Our boss is superior. Our boss-"

"is prob useless little old lady takes advantage of children need love, support respect," Harry said from the doorway.

Sean's heart shot into his throat. He was impressed how much better his speech was coming along. He didn't want him down here. He only wanted Harry to be safe.

The young woman grinned. "Excellent. We have the boyfriend and the nephew. The boss will be so pleased,"

Then it twigged to Sean that they were never going to rob the house. This was actually all about him and Harry and they were probably going to take them hostage or threaten them until Bettie agreed to leave them alone.

Sean admired the stupidity of their boss because he just knew that any threats made against him and Harry would be met with rage, a man hunt and strict retribution.

But Sean admired people's willingness to doom themselves.

Sean stood up. Now that he had some idea of what the two criminals wanted he just needed to break them up and weaken whatever hold the young woman had over the other one.

If he was to act then Sean needed them not to be

a team.

"I know you don't respect the boy over there," Sean said pointing to the young man. "You see him as a pointless burden that your boss made you bring him along. I think he isn't the brilliant tool in the workshop,"

The young woman nodded. "Of course not. I come from a quality background not some council estate where idiots call each other *mate, bro* and *dude,*"

The young man stomped his foot. He was clearly annoyed.

Sean looked at Harry who was extremely beautiful standing there and they just winked at each other.

Sean's pretended his heart pounded. His breathing quickened. He clutched his chest.

Sean hissed and screamed and panicked.

The young woman looked shocked and panicked herself.

Sean collapsed to the sofa. Pretending to have a panic attack. Harry shouted at them.

The young woman dropped the knife.

She rushed to Sean. Leaning over him.

Sean kicked her.

Punching her in the chest.

She flew to the ground.

Sean leapt up. Jumping on top of her.

Sean pinned her down.

The young man whacked Sean in the head.

The young woman threw Sean off her.

Sean jumped up.

The moment he saw the young woman holding Harry in a headlock with the small knife kissing his neck. Sean stopped.

The young man put Sean in a headlock to (a rather pathetic one but still) and Sean just felt like he was a complete and utter failure.

He had put the love of his life in danger and for what. His own insecurities about the corrupt police that had put him in hospital, his own anxiety and God knows whatever concerns he had that made him feel like he was the only one that could protect himself and that no one else cared about him.

Then the living room got a little brighter. No one else seemed to notice and Sean couldn't understand if the bright tones of the living rooms were actually brighter than before but they just felt like they did.

Sean just knew that something was about to happen and he really needed to distract them.

"Your boss doesn't love you you know. She might have found you on the streets or whatever but she actually hates you," Sean said.

The young woman seemed furious. Sean hated the sound of the young man's breathing in his ear.

"And you," Sean said to the young woman. "If your beginnings were so great then why were you on the street to be found?"

The young woman's hand tensed. She gestured she would kill Harry but Sean knew that would only anger her boss.

"I think you were just a jumped-up child that no one wanted and you wanted to get respect from another person that doesn't even love you," Sean said coldly.

The young woman threw Harry onto the sofa. She stormed over to Sean waving the knife about.

"I am loved. The boss loves me. She treasures

me and-"

The front door exploded open.

Sean jumped back.

Smashing the young man into the wall. His head cracked on the wall.

He released Sean.

Sean spun around. Punching the man in the nose.

He collapsed to the ground.

And when Sean looked at where the young woman had been standing, he saw one of the most perfect sights he ever could have wished for, because Graham in his fine black suit was handcuffing the young woman and reading her her rights.

A few moments later after Graham had escorted the young man and woman out of the house, Sean just smiled as a very pregnant Bettie English stumbled through the front door.

Sean had to admit she did look stunningly beautiful in her large black dress that managed to make her massive baby bump seem so stylish and she simply hugged Sean and Harry.

Sean loved the amazing warmth of the hug and he was glad that they had arrived when they did, and more importantly that beautiful Harry was okay.

Then Sean noticed the evil smile on Bettie's face, and Sean looked up at the ceiling and noticed a very small black camera right above his head.

"You knew this would happen," Sean said.

Bettie shrugged as she stumbled over to the armchair.

"Didn't you think it was odd that the kitchen window didn't lock properly?" Bettie asked.

Sean hadn't even noticed.

"That created the perfect opening for them to

come in. I knew you two were smart enough to stay safe until we arrived and you got us the proof we needed," Bettie said.

"Proof what?" Harry asked.

"Two days ago I ran a background check for a government role and it highlighted that criminal gangs were trying to get jobs in the UK Government and someone was helping them,"

Sean just nodded. It was just getting too ridiculous with the Government for words.

"So after some investigating," Bettie said, "me and Graham managed to track down the extra help to an orphanage and homeless shelter in London and the owner, a little old lady I should note, had powerful friends in the government,"

Sean nodded. "This woman was doing favours for her friends by getting the vulnerable children she *cared* for to do her dirty work for her all to protect her criminal friends in the government,"

Bettie nodded.

Sean looked at beautiful Harry who was hugging him and Sean was slightly getting more and more concerned about how thin he was getting, but that was all part of the therapy process.

Sean kissed Harry's soft amazing lips quickly and then pointed to the stairs. It was a little gesture they both did when they knew the other needed to go to sleep.

Sean was never going to have Harry tired when he had a brain therapy day tomorrow, he just loved him too much for that.

Sean was about to follow Harry up when Bettie gently took his hand in hers.

"You did well today you know," Bettie said. "Your mum might not say it or be here, but I am proud of you and love you,"

Sean knew his auntie never understood the power of those words to him, but after hiding he was gay for so many years and all the bad mental health associated with it, being attacked by the people who were meant to protect everyone and now his own parents not seeming to care about him.

Those words meant everything to Sean.

Sean kissed Bettie on the head. "You're going to be an amazing mum,"

Bettie only nodded and she was probably holding back the tears (both in joy but also panic that her life was going to change forever in less than a month) and Sean simply went upstairs.

Sean might have done a great thing today that proved to him he was always more than his anxiety, past and the pain of what had happened. But there was always more to work on in the future.

Right now, he had a beautiful boyfriend to help, love and cherish and a wonderful Auntie to help with a pair of twins coming.

That would probably be a lot for most 21-year-olds to take but Sean honestly couldn't think of a better way to spend his time.

Not a single better way at all.

AUTHOR OF THE ENGLISH BETTIE PRIVATE EYE SERIES

CONNOR WHITELEY

FINDING A ROYAL FRIEND

A BETTIE PRIVATE EYE MYSTERY SHORT STORY

FINDING A ROYAL FRIEND
12:00 pm
8th September 2022
Canterbury, England

Private Eye Bettie English had always liked the royal family in general, and when she had met the Queen a couple of times during her Private Eye work, Bettie had loved their kindness, charm and style even more, even though Bettie purposefully said she was never ever a royalist in the strictest of terms. But she did love them anyway.

Bettie sat at her dark oak desk in her bright white office playing some calming classical music (definitely not her first choice of music) as Bettie was in her large office above the cobblestone high street of Canterbury. Bettie had always loved her office's dark brown wooden walls, cream ceiling and her personal favourite was the mini-bar area tucked away in one corner.

Bettie had always loved working and living and

breathing in Canterbury high street, because she really liked the wonderful sounds of students walking past, talking and shouting about how great their day had been.

All the little bakeries and cafes and restaurants leaked their sensational smells into the air, and even though Bettie had been a vegan since her pregnancy because animal products made her vomit. She still loved the sensational aromas of freshly baked bread, rich juicy pork and the sweetest creamiest cakes she had ever smelt.

Living in Canterbury was amazing.

The mini-bar really helped to make the office feel more luxurious, posh and expensive, all with the added bonus that it really helped to impress brand-new clients whenever they walked in. Bettie might have been a millionaire because of her private eye work, but she preferred to show her skill and wealth in a lot more subtle ways.

The mini-bar was one of them.

Granted the mini-bar was becoming a bit of a pain recently, especially with Bettie being so pregnant and she really, really looking forward to finally giving birth in the next few weeks, but she was such a workaholic that she didn't want to take "real" maternity leave from her Private Eye work so instead she was just working in her office on a bunch of background checks from various government sources and earning a very nice amount of money whilst she waited to give birth.

And Bettie knew that lots of brand-new private eyes hated background checks and believed all the myths about private eyes working grand cases, but that wasn't true in the slightest. The only reason why she had worked a lot in the past was because she had earned herself a reputation for being amazing at her job. And those high-stake cases always tended to find her anyway.

As Bettie was also the president of the British private Eye Federation, after she had been voted in as the new president after all the chaos and stupidity of the last one, David Osborne, she was slowly making changes, giving good people certain roles and making sure that the Federation could survive without her for a few months.

Something she was still a little unsure about.

Especially as because of Bettie banning all the far-left and far-right members of the organisation, she had lost millions of pounds worth of membership fees, sponsors and other political donations from dodgy foreign powers that Bettie had had absolutely no idea invested so much in the Federation for nefarious reasons.

It had only been in the past month that Bettie had realised how fanatically corrupt her beloved Federation and fellow private eyes had been. Something she was desperate to fix but it was her fixing that had meant the Federation was twenty million pounds out of pocket and that number was only growing.

Bettie's computer buzzed a little and Bettie didn't know in the slightest who would be wanting to video chat with her.

Bettie answered it.

She instantly smiled when she saw it was Agent Daniels of MI5, a great, amazing, wonderful man that Bettie and her boyfriend had had the great pleasure of working with a few months back. Bettie had to admit he looked great in his tight well-fitting black suit that framed his face amazingly and he just looked perfect.

That was instantly how Bettie knew something was wrong.

"Agent Daniels," Bettie said, "what do I owe this unexpected pleasure?"

Daniels pretended to smile but Bettie could see that something was paining him.

"What's wrong and I'll put the Federation on it?" Bettie asked.

Daniels shook his head. "In thirty minutes Buckingham Palace will put out a statement saying the Queen in under medication supervision to start preparing the nation for…"

Bettie hated seeing Daniels so choked up and concerned and she instantly knew what was going on.

The Queen was dying.

That realisation slammed into Bettie like a ton of bricks, she had never been a royalist but the Queen was amazing, kind and such a great woman that Bettie couldn't imagine her not being around anymore, but why was Daniels calling her?

"I'm sorry to hear that," Bettie said.

Daniels slowly nodded. "And the Queen has requested something but she knows she cannot ask MI5 or 6 or any government-run security service,"

Bettie leant forward, that was interesting to say the least. Bettie knew that if it was revealed that the Queen had asked the security services, that were funded by taxpayers, to do a personal errand then it risked inflaming and growing the UK's thankfully small republican movement.

Something Bettie really didn't want.

"Miss English," Daniels said, very formally. "The Queen has asked you to find an old friend of hers. She wants to see one of her oldest friends again before she dies,"

Bettie couldn't speak, even the realisation that the Queen was dying made a lump form in her throat.

"We know you're very pregnant and we wouldn't be asking this unless it was critical," Daniels said. "But in 1952 when the newly married Princess was living in Malta and her father had just died,"

Bettie got out a pen and paper from her top desk draw and started making notes.

"The Princess was mugged and attacked by some anti-monarchy English people on holiday in Malta," Daniels said. "The Princess was alone at the time so she didn't have any help but a little girl, aged 13, did intervene and effectively saved the princess from the

English,"

Bettie nodded that was great news.

"When the Princess became Queen the incident was sealed and because of all the new responsibilities, political pressures and more, the Princess and the little girl lost touch. The Queen wants you to find her old friend again if you can," Daniels said.

Bettie just smiled because it was an impossible request and ask, she was extremely pregnant due to give birth any day now, but she so badly wanted to help the Queen so she was going to have to call in all the help she could get.

Then Bettie realised there had to be another reason why Daniels had called her just as her email pinged.

Bettie opened the email from Daniels and it contained all the information she needed to find the little girl, who was now called Sarah Attard, and she had moved to the UK in the late 90s and she was retired now and living somewhere in Rochester, England.

Now Bettie understood why Daniels had called her because Sarah was close enough and thankfully there was an address attached, but Bettie instantly recognised it as the address of a house that burnt down two weeks ago.

The only reason why Bettie knew about it was because her and her boyfriend Graham, a cop, had been in Rochester going out for dinner when the fire happened.

"I'll do my best," Bettie said. "What happens when I find her?"

Daniels smiled and it was great to see him so relieved. "Call me and I'll authorise a helicopter to pick you and Sarah up and we'll fly you to Balmoral to see the Queen,"

Bettie couldn't help my smile that was going to be amazing.

"But Bettie," Daniels said, "the Queen is dying and we really don't know how much longer she has. Time is critical here and it is not on our side,"

Another lump formed in Bettie's throat and she simply nodded ending the video chat.

Bettie took out her phone and made some calls. If she was going to get this done then she really needed help.

And with Graham working on anti-drug operations all week and her sister being next to useless in these sort of situations there was only one person who Bettie could call.

Bettie needed to talk to her nephew. Now.

***

12:40 pm
8th September 2022
Rochester, England

Bettie carefully got out of her nephew's little black car being ever so careful not to knock herself and her very large baby bump at all, Bettie had checked constantly on social media and news sites since the news broke about the Queen and the nation was truly devastated.

Thankfully no one had dared to imagine this was it for the Queen, Bettie felt so guilty and almost burdened by the knowledge but she just had to crack on and find Sarah Attard.

Sean had parked on a slightly sloped road on the edges of the historic city of Rochester with the remains of the flint roman wall close by, the noisy cobblestone high street with all of its Victorian buildings standing proudly, and the massive castle and cathedral being visible over the tops of houses in front of Bettie.

The road they were on wasn't the best that Bettie had ever seen with its massive potholes, little terrace houses with dirty windows and overgrown front gardens.

But Bettie was a lot more interested in the large burnt out remains of a house a little further up the road, that even now still made the air smell of charred wood, destruction and smouldering wreckage.

Of course because the fire had been two weeks ago, Bettie just knew that she was imagining the smell for the most part, but she still hated seeing burnt-down houses.

"Auntie," Sean said, wearing tight blue jeans, a loose grey t-shirt and his very tasteful and great-looking pink highlights in his longish blond hair were starting to grow out ever so slightly, which was a shame because they really did suit him.

Bettie gestured to the house up ahead and she went as quick as she could over to the burnt-out husk of the house, which wasn't easy considering how pregnant she was.

Bettie was really glad that was Sean was here though, him and his boyfriend Harry had been amazing help on other cases, and it was very useful that he could drive now, so she could use him as a family taxi service. And considering him and his boyfriend were living with Bettie and Graham whilst Harry recovered from a brain injury it was the least they could do.

And thankfully Sean was only too happy to help.

"What are you we looking for?" Sean asked.

Bettie wasn't sure exactly as she stared at the exploded-out windows, blackened bricks and Bettie just knew that the inside was completely destroyed. She couldn't even imagine the pain of knowing that all of a person's processions were destroyed in an instant.

"This is the only address Daniels had on Sarah so I'm hoping we'll manage to find some trace of her and where she went," Bettie said.

Sean nodded and as he went over to knock on the door of the house to Bettie's right, she was just horrified that a person's entire life could be destroyed so quickly and easily by something as simple as fire.

But Bettie had a job to do.

Bettie went over to Sarah's next neighbourhood

to her left, which was a very attractive little house with dirty windows, and a messy garden but the front door was bright yellow with little flowers painted on by hand very well.

Bettie knocked on the front door and moments later a little old lady opened the door wearing a little dirty jumper, black trousers and glasses that made the woman definitely look her age.

Bettie almost wanted to gag at the woman's body odour it was so discussing and Bettie had never smelt anything of bad.

"Hi dear," the woman said.

"Hello," Bettie said showing the woman her Private Eye ID, something she had made all Private Eyes have to have under UK law to prove that they were licensed by the Federation.

"Are you looking for Sarah?" the woman asked.

Bettie slowly nodded. It was strange she would just know that.

"Relax dear," the woman said, "two other elderly men came round yesterday looking for her. You look kinder than them though and much more successful than those low lives,"

Bettie bit her lip she really didn't like the sound of that because now she was just worried about why other people were looking for Sarah.

The time seemed too strange.

"What did you tell them?" Bettie asked.

The woman shrugged. "Just that Sarah was a

great neighbour to me and we played blackjack and watched quiz programmes together every Monday, Tuesday and Friday and it broke my heart when she had to move after the fire,"

Bettie smiled, Sarah really did sound like a great neighbour and friend.

"But where did she move to?" Bettie asked.

The woman looked down at the floor. "Um... she said she had a son in Dover that she was moving in with and I was meant to come down and see her next week. You know to see how she was getting on,"

"And don't come back you gay boy!" an elderly man shouted as Sean ran back to his car and a jar of something smashed on the ground behind him.

"Oh I couldn't recommend anyone see Terrance these days. Terrible racist, homophobia and sexist pig you know," the woman said.

Bettie just shook her head. "I cannot stress this enough but it's very important I get to Sarah before these men do. Can I please have that address?"

Bettie hated seeing the little old lady's face turn pale and she slowly nodded as she stood out her little black flip phone and showed Bettie the address.

It wasn't even in Dover but Sarah's son was in a large seaside town close by.

Bettie hugged the little old lady and thanked her for her time and stormed back to Sean's car.

Bettie didn't know what was going on but she just had to get to Whitstable now before the men hunting Sarah got to her.

Because Bettie just knew that only bad things would happen when the men found her.

And Bettie had to find Sarah and take her to Balmoral. She morally didn't have another choice.

Time was definitely running out now.

***

1:45 pm

8th September 2022

Whitstable, England

Bettie seriously hated the bad traffic and how long all of this was taking, the Queen was dying and Bettie would feel like such an utter failure if she didn't find Sarah in time. Things were getting really bad and Bettie was definitely starting to feel the pressure.

Thankfully Sarah's son lived in an apartment above the restaurant him and his wife owned along the seafront so Sean had parked the car as quickly as he could and Bettie and him were walking as quickly as they could along the seafront.

Bettie had always liked Whitstable seafront with its wide concrete sea wall that formed the pathway for tens upon tens of people to walk on, the very wide range of restaurants serving the freshest of seafood lining one side of the seafront and the stunningly crystal blue sea on the other side.

The air was crisp, salty and so refreshing that Bettie really loved it but they had to find Sarah's son.

"Where's the restaurant?" Sean asked.

"It should be up ahead," Bettie said.

After a few more moments of walking Bettie saw a very large black restaurant with tons of nautical theme decorations on the outside and it was packed. Bettie could smell the freshly fried fish and chips and other wonderful seafood delights from metres away.

Bettie almost wanted to be sick because seafood was another food group that her pregnant body hated to smell, touch or eat, but Bettie just had to manage.

Bettie rolled her eyes at the very short line and supposed it might serve their purpose better if they at least waited in line instead of being rude and forcing their way into the restaurant.

Bettie and Sean waited in line with three young families and an adult couple in front of them. Bettie was going to give the line five minutes to get to them before she forced her way towards the women seating everyone in the restaurant.

"How goes the Federation's money crisis?" Sean asked.

Bettie laughed. She really did love having Sean and Harry living with them because they were some of the best and smartest and most loving people she had ever known but they definitely had a habit of listening to "private" conversations between Bettie and her inner circle in the evenings.

One of the young families were seated.

"Awful," Bettie said. "I'm pouring tons of my millions into the Federation to keep it afloat and I suspect the Federation will be bankrupted by the end of the year because of the stupidity of David,"

Sean hugged her. "You're clever everything will be fine,"

Bettie really hoped he was right.

The other couples and young families got seated because they were part of a massive group and Bettie waved at the young woman who was seating everyone.

Bettie showed the woman her Private Eye ID. "I must speak to Sarah Attard please,"

The young woman gave Bettie a weak smile and waved Bettie to get closer.

"That's impossible Miss English," the woman said. "Last night we had a break-in and this morning when I arrived Mr and Ms Attard were gone and there was a lot of blood on the floor,"

Bettie felt Sean put his hands on her shoulder and rubbed it gently. None of this was good and this was the last thing that Bettie needed.

Sarah and her son were kidnapped and now they had no leads on where they were and each second the Queen was one second closer to death.

Not ideal but Bettie needed to be more demanding and proactive now for Sarah would definitely be joining the Queen in death she feared.

"Show me the apartment now," Bettie said firmly.

The young woman shyly nodded and led Bettie and Sean into the restaurant.

Bettie just hoped Sarah and her son were still

alive if the men had taken them.

***

1:50 pm
8th September 2022
Whitstable, England

Bettie was completely shocked as she went into the gutted apartment belonging to Sarah's son with its smashed-up wooden dining table, ripped-up sofas along the back wall with a stunning sea view and even the smart TV had been knocked over but what really caught Bettie's attention were the massive drag marks in dark rich red blood coming towards the door.

"What did the police say?" Bettie asked as her and Sean and the young woman went into the apartment.

The young woman just stood by the door not daring to come into the apartment but Bettie and Sean were used to this sight and crime scenes so they hardly had a problem with it.

Sean went into one of the smaller rooms that shot off the much large living table with the sofa, TV and dining table. Bettie was fairly sure Sean was looking through the kitchen area.

Bettie went over to the smart TV.

"The police said there was nothing they could do," the young woman said. "They tried to find fingerprints and other evidence but they said everything had… washed or something,"

Bettie nodded but if the men were smart enough to wash things down that would get rid of their fingerprints then why not clean up the drag marks in blood.

"Auntie," Sean said from the kitchen. "If Sarah's son runs a seafood restaurant then why is there no fish in his fridge and plenty of EpiPens in draws?"

Bettie just looked at the young woman. That was a great question because surely a chef that loved seafood so much would be creating dishes and experimenting with seafood in his private apartment, and surely he wouldn't be working with shellfish or other seafood if he needed an EpiPen because of allergies.

"Unless the EpiPen belonged to Sarah," Bettie said as she went over to the young woman who was looking at the floor. "And what really happened this morning?"

Sean came out of the kitchen and folded his arms as he stood next to Bettie.

"We know this apartment is off," Bettie said. "Your boss is famous in Whitstable for his love of seafood so why would his shellfish-allergic mother come here? Or tell other people she was?"

Bettie really didn't like this young woman hiding things from her.

"It wasn't meant to go like this," the young woman said. "My boss had called his mum all concerned because some men were looking for her. Sarah had been out when the fire started and the police ruled it an accident but it wasn't,"

Bettie just nodded, that would actually make a lot of sense.

Sean stepped forward. "Then Sarah told your boss and, yourself, where she was really going but made you both promise to say and act like she was here,"

Bettie nodded. "So your boss got rid of his fish and shellfish and Sarah probably sent him a bunch of old EpiPens just so if the restaurant was being watched it would look like he was preparing for the arrival of his mother,"

The young woman nodded.

"But that doesn't explain where's the wife is and what happened to your boss," Bettie said.

The young woman leant across the doorframe and shrugged. "I don't know. I guess that men had come after him and took him and his wife,"

Bettie just looked at Sean. If there was any chance that they were going to get Sarah, her son and his wife back safe and alive then Bettie had to know where Sarah really was.

Sean nodded to Bettie as he hugged the young woman gently.

"Please," Bettie said. "Just tell us where Sarah is. We can help her and her family we just need to know where,"

Sean stepped away from the young woman and Bettie really hoped the young woman trusted them enough.

"She's in Canterbury. There's a small hotel on the

outskirts that she went to," the young woman said.

Bettie and Sean rushed out the apartment.

"Thank you!" Bettie shouted as her and Sean raced to find Sarah before the men got to her first.

And probably killed her for some reason.

***

3:20 pm
8th September 2022
Canterbury, England

Bettie wasn't messing about in the slightest as her and Sean walked across the large car park towards a very small bright blue hotel that only had ten rooms with trees lining the car park as the wind lashed and slashed at them.

Bettie and Sean were about to go in through the large glass door when she noticed out of all the five cars parked at the hotel only one was dripping something onto the concrete below.

Bettie focused on the large black SUV that was dripping something and she went over to it. Sean knelt down on the ground and nodded at Bettie.

She just knew that it was blood and as much as she didn't like breaking into cars, if there was an injured person or dead body in the car then she had to know.

"I'll open the car," Sean said.

Bettie nodded and got out her lockpicks that weren't designed for cars but they were just as effective in her experience. And Sean started to pick the car.

Bettie looked around making sure no one was watching. She seriously doubted the security cameras above the glass doors of the hotel actually worked anyway.

A few moments later Sean had the car doors pop open and he unlocked the boot.

Bettie pushed open the boot and gasped as she saw a man and woman laying there with massive gashes to their head and each of them were tightly holding each other and their chests.

Each trying to apply pressure to the stab wounds.

Sean shook his head when he saw them and immediately called for an ambulance.

Bettie pressed each of her hands firmly on the stab wounds of Sarah's son and his wife and they hissed but Bettie was a lot more concerned about Sarah.

"Who did this?" Bettie asked.

Sarah's son fell unconscious and the wife started crying. She wasn't going to get answers from either of them.

"Sean," Bettie said firmly.

He came back over.

"Place your hands over their stab wounds and apply pressure like you did with Harry on the night of the attack," Bettie said.

It might have been harsh to remind him of the attack but Bettie didn't have time and Sean probably understood.

"And don't let go until the ambulance arrives," Bettie said. "And call Daniels,"

He nodded.

Sean took over from Bettie and she kissed him quickly on the cheek and went into the hotel through the large glass doors.

Bettie hated the chemically smell of the small bright white reception area with fake plants everywhere and no one was on duty and the dark blue carpets looked awful in this place.

"Help me!" a woman shouted.

Bettie hid behind a large fake palm tree near the entrance.

"Shut up bitch," a man said.

Bettie saw three large muscular men, clearly English, dragging Sarah who was a small elderly woman towards the door.

Bettie stepped out from her cover and stood firmly in front of the glass doors.

"I cannot let you leave," Bettie said.

The three men laughed at her. And Bettie really focused on their awful artic white beards, fragile frames and then it all made sense to Bettie.

"You're the men who attacked the Queen in 1952," Bettie said.

Bettie was shocked but it made perfect sense. The men were clearly in their nineties but they would have been teenagers when they attacked the Queen in Malta and they had clearly looked after their bodies to be this capable after so long.

Just like the Queen and Sarah assembly had.

Each of the three men whipped out a knife and gestured they would kill Sarah if Bettie didn't leave.

"You're going to kill her anyway," Bettie said. "And why do all this? Why kill the woman that stopped you from killing the Queen seventy years ago?"

The three men laughed.

The man holding Sarah spat at Bettie. "You see what the Monarch's doing. Costing British taxpayers millions of pounds. The Monarchy must die and all those that support them must die too,"

Bettie really wanted to point out whilst 2022 or 2021 (she never had paid attention to the year) had been the first time the monarchy had cost the taxpayer over £100 million pounds, the Uk still had a government that had written over billions of pounds of fraud for no reason, gave million-pound contracts to their friends in exchange for faulty goods and used so much taxpayer money to line their own pockets.

Why was that right but the monarchy wasn't?

But political differences didn't seem like a good idea here.

"You're monsters!" Sarah shouted.

"Shut up!" the man holding her shouted. Slapping her across the face.

Bettie took a few steps forward. "You don't want to do this. You haven't killed anyone yet and you have only injured a couple of people,"

The three men laughed.

"Stupid woman," the man holding Sarah said. "We know what ya trying to do. It wouldn't work,"

The three men raised their knives.

Bettie rushed forward. The three men stared at Bettie.

The large glass doors smashed open.

Everyone looked at the broken glass.

Smoke grenades flew through the air.

The three men were confused.

Bettie shot forward.

Whacking the man holding Sarah in-between the legs.

He released Sarah.

Bettie grabbed her. Throwing her to one side.

Two men grabbed Bettie's arms pulling them in opposite directions.

The last raised the knife.

He was going to kill Bettie.

Bullets screamed through the air.

Heads exploded.

Blood painted Bettie's face.

As the three corpses fell to the ground Bettie had to get to Sarah, she rushed over to Sarah and threw the elderly lady over her shoulder. Bettie's twins kicked in excitement inside her.

Men and women in full body armour stormed into the reception area, their faces completely covered and Bettie just ignored them.

Bettie went outside the hotel and Sean took Sarah from her and gently threw her over his shoulder.

Bettie smiled as Agent Daniels in his tight black suit waved her and Sean over.

Daniels led them into a wide open field at the back of the hotel and a black helicopter activated to take them away.

"Who are you?" Sarah asked as her weak body struggled in Sean's grip as they all hurried towards the helicopter.

"Bettie English Private Eye, my nephew Sean and Agent Daniels MI5. The woman you saved in 52 wants to see you before she dies,"

Bettie was waiting for Sarah to start punching Sean's back or something but she just smiled.

"Fucking hell young man start running," Sarah said.

And as Bettie, Daniels and Sean with Sarah over his shoulder ran towards the helicopter Bettie just hoped beyond hope that the Queen would still be alive by the time they got to Balmoral in Scotland.

Bettie just couldn't fail.

***

6:32 pm

8th September 2022

Balmoral Estate, Scotland

Bettie had actually forgotten had slow compared to planes Helicopters were but she was rather amazed that the helicopter (because it was a military one) hadn't needed to refill at all during the journey.

Bettie had always absolutely loved the amazing highlands of Scotland, and whilst she really hoped Scotland gain its independence from the corruption of Westminster and London, she was so glad to be here in beautiful Scotland for this very special occasion.

Bettie was sitting against an icy cold window with Sarah and Sean next to her in a very uncomfortable seat as Daniels and the pilot continued to descend into the Balmoral estate, Bettie loved seeing the immensely wide open green fields of the estate and very tall pine and oak and other types of trees almost rise up to greet them.

Even though Bettie was in the helicopter she could still smell the delightful crisp refreshing piney air as the helicopter landed on the thick green grass with the Balmoral mansion just tens of metres away.

And it really did look like the most beautiful and perfect stately manor Bettie had ever seen, it looked right out of something from Downton Abbey.

But as the helicopter doors slid open and Bettie stepped onto the thick cold grass, she instantly knew that something was wrong and they were far too late, and judging by Sarah's smiling face it was only Bettie that had picked up on the change of tension in the air.

Bettie looked at Balmoral mansion and she frowned as a long life of ten servants, both men and women, in fine black suits and uniforms walked towards them in perfect step with each other, she just knew that she had been right.

Daniels took Sarah towards the servants and Sean just wrapped a thin youthful arm around Bettie, and she just rested her head on his shoulders.

"She's dead isn't she?" Sean asked.

Bettie felt a lump form in her throat and she just nodded.

The Queen of the UK and commonwealth was dead after an amazing 96 years of her life and even more amazing 70 years of constant love, service and dedication to her duty as Queen.

Even as Bettie stood there just watching Daniels and Sarah talk to the servants that were teary and looked just as upset as Bettie felt, she really wondered if she would still be doing her duty as a private eye at 96 years old.

Probably not, because as much as she loved being a private eye, the President of the Federation and newly expecting mother, things couldn't last forever, and at some point Bettie just knew she would have to choose what she really wanted in life.

But somehow the amazing Queen had managed to keep focused on duty, service and doing everything she could for this country. And Bettie damn well respected her for that.

Sarah's cries and screams of emotional pain ripped through the entire estate, and Bettie almost wanted to join her because she felt like such a failure but Bettie already knew that she had done a lot of good today.

As Bettie and Sean watched the most upset servant hug and try to reassure and grieve *with* Sarah about their own traumatic loss, Bettie just watched as the oldest of the servants slowly make her way over to Bettie holding a scroll of some sort.

Whilst the oldest servant made her way over, Bettie was rather amazed at how upset the Queen's workers were, because she had always heard stories of how much of a great sensational boss the Queen was, but to actually see how much her staff loved her.

That was something else entirely.

"Miss Bettie English, Private Eye and Madame President of the British Private Eye Federation," the woman said as poshly as Bettie ever could have imagined one of the Queen's servants to talk.

Bettie stopped leaning on Sean and stood up perfectly straight.

"Her Majesty wished me to give you this on your arrival," the woman said. "It was one of the last acts of business she ever did during her glorious life and before she made sure she told each of her family members how much she loved them,"

Bettie forced herself not to cry. It was amazing that the Queen had forced herself to do something for Bettie before she died, but Bettie just had a feeling that was the sort of amazing woman the late Queen was.

The woman passed Bettie the scroll and she

opened it.

Bettie was amazed that it was a short letter to Bettie personally from the Queen informing Bettie that because she was just a good private eye, one so good that even the Queen had heard of her and her dedication to the UK. The Queen was officially requesting the new King to knight Bettie, and the Queen was gifting the Federation one million pounds to help them out.

Because apparently the Queen admired Bettie's courage and even though the Queen never ever wanted the royal family to have political power again, she would have liked to imagine she would have had the same amount of courage as Bettie in that situation with banning the far-left and right from the Federation.

Bettie felt her eyes turn wet as she handed the scroll to Sean, and she simply bowed to the servant and the servant smiled before heading back to her friends and Sarah and Daniels.

Bettie just leant against the icy coldness of the helicopter as the news of everything sunk in and she had to admit that even though she had technically failed to bring Sarah to the Queen before she sadly died, Bettie with the amazing help of Sean had still managed to do some incredible things today.

They had saved the lives of Sarah, her son and his wife from certain death, they had stopped three ninety-year-old men from spreading their hate and criminal views onto others that they were bound to have done after the killings, and most importantly Bettie had actually done exactly what the Queen had wanted.

Because Bettie, Sean and Sarah had all been here when it mattered most and they had protected the innocent.

And now the Queen was sadly dead, Bettie just knew that tonight was going to be a sad night, but that wasn't what the Queen would have wanted. She would have wanted a great night filled with stories, laughter and true friendship and as Daniels waved her and Sean over to them, Bettie just knew that was exactly what she was going to get.

And that was definitely going to be the greatest of endings to a very strange, dangerous and sad day, because how many people could honesty say they had been to the Queen's Balmoral estate as a guest.

Bettie couldn't think of a single person, and that just excited her way more than she ever wanted to admit.

BETTIE PRIVATE INVESTIGATOR SHORT STORY
COLLECTION VOLUME 3

KEY TO BIRTH IN THE PAST
15th September 2022
Canterbury, England

Being a Private Eye back in the day was a rather wonderful thing that Bettie English absolutely loved to do. There was nothing in the entire world like chasing down criminals on the cold rocky slopes of valleys in Yorkshire, smelling the sweet scent of water passing through an apple orchard in Kent whilst delivering top-secret information to a secret government base, and Bettie just loved the sweet salty taste of cotton-candy on her tongue as she watched an unfaithful husband at a festival.

But all that was about to change.

Bettie laid on a perfectly comfortable and warm blue hospital bed with some very thin (almost impractically thin) bedsheets pulled over her and the cold white metal of the bed frame rested against the back of her head. She had been a lot lower on the bed before with each contraction she had moved herself higher and higher onto the bed.

After nine amazing months of pregnancy, Bettie was finally going to give birth to her wonderful twins that had actually given her a lot of joy so far, and hopefully that would only continue.

Bettie smiled at her nephew Sean with his blue jeans, white t-shirt and blond hair with stylish pink highlights running through it. He stood perfectly straight as he rested against the sterile white walls of the hospital room, and his boyfriend Harry was sitting on a wooden chair next to him.

Bettie was really pleased to have them both with her because if anything, in recent months both of them had basically became her children. Especially with Sean's parents more or less kicking him and Harry out after they were attacked and Harry had sustained a brain injury.

Bettie wasn't sure if she was ever going to be able to forgive her sister for that, but truth be told with the twins coming, Bettie was just glad for the support.

"Don't break my fingers again babe,"

Bettie just laughed as she rested her hands on her baby bump and watched her sexy beautiful boyfriend Detective Graham Adams walk back into the hospital room with three fingers on his left hand fixed up.

It wasn't even like Bettie had meant to scream and react so much during one of the contractions. She had just focused on how the twins were acting inside her, it was only when Graham started screaming that she realised she had managed to break three of his fingers.

A very eventful start to the evening.

"Sorry I'm late everyone," Bettie's sister Phryne said as she strolled in wearing a very wet raincoat and carrying four to-go coffee mugs.

Bettie loved the delightful smell of the rich bitter

coffee that filled the entire room and she was more than looking forward to the kids coming out, just so she could have a cup of coffee again.

"Auntie," Sean said, ignoring his mother. Harry just hugged Sean tighter. "I've never asked how you two met?"

Graham just laughed, and Bettie just smiled. Their love story was one of… an interesting start that definitely had a long road to this moment, but it was sort of beautiful in a way.

Bettie hardly had anything better to do with the doctors saying it was at least another 30 minutes before the babies were due. So she might as well tell her family the in-detail version of how they met.

Bettie just looked at Graham. "I'll start?"

Graham gingerly held her hand and kissed it. "Be my guest,"

Bettie couldn't believe how excited she felt about telling her family the crazy, criminal and spectacular story about how she met the love of her life.

***

12th October 2010

Hertfordshire, England

23-year-old Bettie English had only been out of university for six months after doing an absolutely awful and god-awful accounting degree. She had no idea whatsoever why she allowed that mother of hers to get her to do an accounting degree. It was rather easy in a way but Bettie hated the numbers and how the companies basically made you a corporate slave.

She wasn't a slave to anything.

Thankfully it wasn't long until she discovered the British Private Eye Federation and it did sound pretty cool being a private eye, so she went for it.

Completed a bunch of impossible training and somewhat managed to get accepted.

Even now Bettie was surprised at how impossible the training was but that was why the Federation was so respected, loved and adored by the investigative community all over the world. It was so hard to get membership only the best made it.

Bettie stood outside a massive clay-red brick wall right outside an immense country estate that was just so typical of Hertfordshire in the midlands of England.

Bettie had always loved the countryside but this was a little too far for her. She was literally standing on a cobblestone road that was supposed to add an extra layer of poshness to the estate but it really didn't.

But that was about as fancy as it got, Bettie was hardly pleased with the miles upon miles of flat open fields with luscious green grass that blew so elegantly in the cool gentle wind.

When Bettie was a kid she might have liked this but she had a job to do now.

As a newly qualified Private Eye, Bettie had to complete hundreds of background checks to serve as a little probation and it was only because her checks were done quickly and effectively, and that the Federation had decided to test her with her first case.

She needed to Serve Papers to a wealthy businessman because he had apparently been involved in manipulating the financial markets, causing tons of businesses and people to lose their savings and he had ruined a lot of lives.

Easy?

Bettie was definitely going to make sure on future cases that she actually researched the places she was going to first of all. Because this place was impossible to get into and she had tried to ring the doorbell on the massive black wooden gates.

They rejected to see her.

But Bettie needed this job more than anything else in the entire world right now because if she failed, she would never be accepted into the Federation fully, she would never be respected and she would be doomed to be a poor private eye for the rest of her life.

Her professional career depended on this.

Even though Bettie couldn't see the estate because the brick walls with barred-wires on top were so tall. She just couldn't understand why someone would want to go to this extremes to protect themselves, and this house was in the middle of nowhere.

Bettie went straight over to the brick wall and ran her fingers across the cold surface. She had hoped to be able to climb it but the surface was far too smooth for her.

The sound of a car driving up slowly made Bettie roll her eyes. The last thing she needed was to get caught or something.

"Excuse me Miss," someone said.

Bettie slowly turned to look at the awfully beaten-up black car that had stopped a few metres from her and there was an elderly woman looking at her.

She didn't look good enough to have the rich and wealth of the person she was looking for, but maybe she could be useful.

"Who are you?" the elderly woman asked.

"A tourist passing through but I'm a little-" Bettie said.

"Really?" the elderly woman asked. "I think you wanna serve the master his court papers,"

Bettie was definitely going to need to become a better liar. She had so much to learn about being a private eye that it was infuriating and exciting.

"I'm sorry about lying," Bettie said, this woman seemed to be nice enough so she wanted to play it nicely.

"I'm the Master's chief of staff, Layla Winston and please leave," she said.

Bettie forced herself not to react, all she wanted to do was serve the court papers so the Federation would properly respect her. She needed this job more than anything.

Then Layla simply drove off again. No doubt she was going to tell her Master so that was just annoying.

Bettie started following Layla's car down the cobblestone road and within a few moments she watched two strong muscular men standing outside the large black wooden gates to the estate as Layla drove inside.

The two men glared at her.

Damn it. The two men hadn't been there before, this was quickly getting worse and worse.

Bettie was going to fail and she was never ever going to be able to get respect and get all the good jobs as a private eye.

She was doomed.

***

12th October 2010

Hertfordshire, England

Detective Graham Adams had never ever liked private eyes. They were the worst type of scum in the entire world because they were clueless, annoying and they were just so useless.

So when Graham had gotten the call about some woman private eye lurking around his target's estate, it just annoyed him. Why couldn't these useless private eyes just stay away and let the real police sort out the crimes.

Graham drove down the little cobblestone road that was definitely far too narrow for his large black land rover with large oak trees lining the road. Their strangely shaped leaves falling in the autumn breeze and dirtying up his windshield.

The only benefit about driving in the autumn was that Hertfordshire had a wonderful crispness to the air along with subtle hints of pine, oak and a freshness from something that Graham couldn't identify.

It didn't take long for Graham to see the massively tall brick walls of the estate, and this was why he had travelled up from Kent Police to help the National Taskforce take down this particular businessman.

Whilst the newspapers and other media reports had only cared to focus on Mr Albert Natt's financial manipulations, Graham knew that he was guilty of a lot more. Albert had also had a hand in three murders, the collapse of two major banks and had links to funding communist terror attacks all over the world.

All Graham had wanted to do was drive into the estate and arrest Albert there and then, but because of the stupid law no one could simply charge into the estate and no one could give him the legal papers.

Apparently the police and Crown Prosecution Service had tried hundreds of different ways. From delivering the papers to lawyers to Albert's family to delivering them through the post. But each time Albert's lawyers simply claimed the papers were never delivered.

It was impossible.

And there was even talk about the Crown Prosecution Service reaching out to the so-called British Private Eye Federation. It was a completely stupid organisation made up of wannabe cops that were just as clueless as the people he arrested most days.

He just hoped this stupid woman wasn't part of that awful hobbyist club, but he just knew she was.

A few seconds later, Graham slowed down his car to a stop and looked at the tall woman in her black trench coat, high heels and long black hair just stare at him as she stood in front of the black gates.

Graham took out his badge and waved her over.

The woman hardly seemed impressed but that had just confirmed his beliefs about private eyes. They were all so cocky, ignorant and awful people that had no respect for the law.

But as the woman walked over to Graham's car, he was just flat out stunned at how beautiful and sexy she was. Graham loved her amazingly soft, sexy lifeful hair that all Graham wanted to do was run his fingers through it.

Even her face looked so soft, beautiful and stunning. She looked like she needed to be on the cover of Vogue or something and not in the woods pretending to be a private eye, she was so beautiful.

And there was just something in the confidence and the way that she walked, it was like she knew exactly where she was going. She looked like she owned the entire land and Graham almost felt like he was the trespasser.

She was stunning.

Instead of the woman walking over to his side and standing outside Graham's car window, the woman had the arrogance to simply walk round the other side of the land rover and board his car.

How dare she.

Graham had to admit as she sat in the passenger seat, she looked even more stunning up close and Graham seriously loved the delightful hints of grapefruit, lemon and oranges that radiated off her.

"Bettie English Private Eye at your service detective," the hot woman said.

Graham had no idea how she had guessed he was a detective, his badge only said he was a cop, but it was just his luck. The only woman he had found attractive was a private eye, the worst sort of people.

"I presume you want to know why I'm here," Bettie said, not as a question.

Graham shrugged. "I know you're here on a little pretend mission. Leave the police work to the cops or I will arrest you no matter how beautiful you are,"

The moment those last words left his mouth he felt like such an idiot. He might have had been about the same age as this Bettie woman and rapidly rose through the ranks to Detective but he was always professional, calm and collective around criminals.

But why was he being so unprofessional in front

of her?

"You aren't so bad yourself detective," Bettie said.

Graham just grinned and forced himself to look away. He couldn't focus on that sexy woman and think straight.

"You need to leave and personally just give up on the Private Eye stuff. It won't get you anywhere in life and you're just making a fool of yourself," Graham said.

He had never heard a woman go deadly silent before and he looked back over at her, and he wasn't sure as he stared into her narrow, cold brown eyes and furious looking face if he should have been scared or what.

After a few moments Bettie laughed and popped open the land rover door.

"Tell me detective if you weren't such a jackass you cops might have delivered the court papers instead of having a *bum* like me to do it," Bettie said.

Graham was about to say something when Bettie slammed the door and stomped back down the cobblestone.

As much as Graham wanted to leave she was trying to do a good thing and if she was successful then she would help him too.

He just had no idea how to help someone like a private eye.

The very worst sort of people.

***

15th September 2022

Canterbury, England

"Wait you hated private eyes?" Sean asked

Graham.

Bettie couldn't believe actually hearing how much her boyfriend hated her at first. It was one thing to experience it and know of it throughout the other times they had met before they started dating the first time, but to hear it.

It was something else.

Bettie hissed in pain as another contraction pulsed and corkscrewed through her, and she was really looking forward to these twins coming out. And she was more than excited about getting off this hospital bed with the stupidly thin blue bed sheets and getting home to a real bed.

"Yea not my best moment," Graham said, blowing Bettie a kiss.

Bettie smiled and shook her head. She did love this man and he had actually proved to be a very capable helper over the years, something she had no doubt would have horrified the 2010-Graham.

And that was a funny idea all by itself.

"Let's continue," Bettie said.

***

12th October 2010

Hertfordshire, England

Bettie flat out hated stupid cops. She had heard about their stupidity on her private eye training but to actually see it and experience it in real life was beyond pathetic.

She hated cops and she was definitely never ever going to date one. They were just too stupid for words.

Bettie stood directly in front of the large black wooden gates and this was the only way into the estate house, and the two men acting as guards stared intently at her. Like she was actually a danger.

Bettie stared at them back, trying not to show them that her stomach was tightening into a painful knot and she didn't actually know what to do. Her entire professional career depended on getting inside and she was failing.

She had never been a violent person but Bettie was starting to wonder whether it might be worth attacking these two people and just breaking inside.

Bettie looked back over at the land rover that was still parked there with that cute(ish) cop with that amazing body, handsome face and stunning eyes she just wanted to stare into all day.

She waved him over.

Bettie went over to the two guards. "Let me in,"

The two guards laughed at her.

"What's going on?" Graham asked, he had clearly run over judging by the panting.

Bettie pretended to look all upset and almost threw herself on Graham for sympathy. At least her childhood acting lessons weren't going to waste.

"These horrible men won't let me in. These men were abusing me and I just want to see my father,"

Bettie almost laughed at last the comment but she didn't dare. She was hoping not to fool Graham but at least make the guards a bit more likely to let them in.

"You're Victoria Natt?" the guards asked.

Bettie stood up perfectly straight. "Of course I am and this is my friend. He's a wealthy investor,".

Bettie loved how hard Graham was trying not to look scared. It probably went against every single rule in the cop playbook, but she wasn't a cop. She was a private eye and a good one at that.

The guards looked Graham up and down, and one of them took out a walkie-talkie from his back pocket.

"Master, your daughter has bought an investor with her," he said into it.

"She isn't my daughter but the man looks rich. Just bring them both inside and he'll deal with them," a man replied through the talkie.

Bettie had to agree with Graham's concerned look that she just felt like she had dug them into a massive whole that she wasn't sure how to get out of.

She just hoped that she wasn't going to put an innocent man in harm's way.

Graham was far too cute for that.

***

12th October 2010

Hertfordshire, England

Graham was seriously impressed at this amazingly sexy woman he was walking next to. She was smart as a whip, smelt amazing and maybe not all private eyes were as silly as each other.

"Wait here for a moment," the guards said as one before they left.

But he was not impressed in the slightest that Bettie had gotten the two guards to lead them into a large spacious room with shiny brown walls with fine art, stuffed animals and other typical spoils of the rich hanging so proudly on the walls like those were the items that his judges would judge him on.

Graham just knew that Albert was that deluded. Albert would only ever be judged on his crimes, not his power and influence.

The only other items of note, not that Graham

was brave enough to look into them, was an oversized brown desk with small piles of legal documents on top and a ritualistic dagger rested in the very centre of the desk.

Graham couldn't believe how much he hated this room considering it could only be described as the pinnacle of selfish richness.

"Here," Bettie said as she started to look at the legal documents.

Graham hated how private eyes just helped themselves. As a cop he couldn't just look at whatever he pleased and take it into evidence.

These private eyes were dangerous laws onto themselves.

"Stop that," Graham said going on to her.

Bettie pointed to a small pile of documents closest to Graham. It was probably a gesture telling him to start looking, but he couldn't. It was against the rules.

"If you don't start looking you might lose something for your investigation," Bettie said.

Graham loved how mischievous she was.

"How do you know I was investigating Albert?" Graham asked.

Bettie shrugged. "Everyone wants to nail Albert and you wouldn't have helped me if you weren't,"

Damn it. She was right. He had only met her less than an hour and she was already making him do things and bend rules for her, something he never would have done for anyone else before.

She was just too beautiful to say no to.

Graham started to look through the small pile of documents next to him and quickly realised that these were flight documents. They were dated for today travelling to countries that didn't have an extradition treaty with the UK.

Albert was going on the run. And he never would have known that without this beautiful woman.

Someone reached over Graham and picked up the ritualistic knife.

Graham spun around and instinctively stepped in front of Bettie when he saw a large elderly man in a posh suit was pointing the knife straight at his chest.

He wasn't going to let Albert hurt Bettie.

"You two are causing me a lot of trouble," Albert said. "Two of my drivers have already cancelled me and now I'm having to be smuggled by my mere cleaner to get to the airport,"

Graham was glad he was suffering a little, it was nothing compared to the thousands of people that were suffering because of him, but every bit of suffering helped.

Albert gestured them to move away from the desk with a few shakes of the knife. Graham complied, Bettie did not.

He loved how defiant she was but this wasn't the time.

Bettie simply folded her arms. "You are many things Albert Natt but you are not a killer, and why let us in?"

Albert laughed. "I needed to get you two troublemakers out of my hair and I want to offer you both a million pounds to leave me alone,"

Graham would have loved that sort of money, he would be able to help out his family, donate to charities and actually make a difference in the world. But he was a cop first and foremost and Bettie didn't even react.

She took a step closer to Albert. Graham did the same.

"You really think you can bride us," Bettie said.

Albert pointed the knife at her and Graham felt his stomach tense. He took another few steps closer. He had to be ready.

Bettie took out the court papers and offered them to him.

Albert just laughed. Hard.

Bettie lunched forward.

Graham rushed over.

Bettie tackled Albert to the ground.

She was going to arrest him.

Graham went to help.

Albert slapped Bettie. She fell off him.

Albert kicked Graham in the stomach.

Graham staggered back.

The two men serving as guards walked in and went towards Bettie and Graham wrapping their arms around them so they couldn't escape.

This was not what Graham needed. Especially as Graham had the most smelliest guard he had ever had.

"You're such an idiot," Graham said to Bettie, hoping to annoy someone enough that the guards' grip would weaken.

Bettie laughed. "Yea like you could do anything better you pig,"

"Typical private eye always name-calling because you're too pathetic yourself,"

"Fuck you cop. I wouldn't be here if you weren't so useless,"

Graham saw how amused and distracted the guards and Albert were.

He stomped his foot down. Bettie did the same.

The guards expected it.

They punched Graham and Bettie in the face.

They both collapsed to the ground.

Pain radiated from Graham's nose, heating up his face, this was going from worst to worst. He never should have gotten involved in stupid private eye business.

"Master," an elderly woman who was presumably the one smuggling Albert to the airport.

"One moment Layla," Albert said as he waved the guards to go and Layla just stood there behind Albert.

Albert walked over to Graham. The point of the ritualistic knife pressed against his throat. Graham didn't even react.

"All I tried to do was make myself rich. Know I destroyed a lot of lives, funded a lot of terror but that only allowed me to make more money, so your efforts to arrest me are pointless. The moment I leave this country I will be free," Albert said.

Bettie laughed hard. "Pathetic really. You claim to be powerful but if you were really you have enough money and power to buy your safety here,"

Graham didn't want to tell her that was exactly what he had been doing for the past year, but those friends within the UK Government had turned against him.

"Good bye detective," Albert said.

Graham grabbed the knife.

Albert kicked Graham in the balls. Pain shot through his body.

Albert grabbed him by the throat.

He prepared to kill Graham.

A foot smashed into Albert's head.

He fell to the ground not moving.

Graham felt Bettie hug him and help him get up. He wanted to hug Bettie back but he pulled her off him and simply looked down at Albert.

It was clear that Bettie had kicked him in the head and judging by the sheer amount of blood pumping out of it, almost like Bettie had popped a blood filled balloon, Albert was most certainly dead.

Graham just folded his arms.

This was going to be a hell of a lot of paperwork.

***

12th October 2010

Hertfordshire, England

A few hours later, Bettie had absolutely no idea if that hot sexy detective had noticed she was still here actually sitting in his very uncomfortable black Land Rover instead of going home. But she was pleased to be here, as much as she acted like she found his car comfortable, she was so lying.

And she was more than pleased as she watched the oak leaves fall off the trees lining the cobblestone road in the autumn breeze, that was still here.

All she wanted to do was talk to that hot sexy detective a final time, maybe thank him and maybe ask him to dinner.

Bettie had to admit he was a real cock about his attitudes towards so-called stupid private eyes, but she could see that he was a good man trying to enforce law and order into a wonderfully chaotic world.

The driver's door opened and Graham just

huffed when he saw her.

"Do you have any idea how much paperwork you have caused me?" he asked.

Bettie shrugged. That was definitely another great benefit about being a private eye, and not a real cop, she didn't have to do even half the amount of paperwork. She could just solve cases, have fun and keep the world safe without as many forms.

"But thanks," Graham said. "I know you didn't have to save my life. Thank you,"

That was probably one of the stupid things Bettie had ever heard. Of course she had to save his life, he was a good man, an innocent and it was just normal to save people. She wouldn't let a hot man die for love or money.

"Do I need to travel back to Kent with you for a statement?" Bettie asked smiling.

Graham threw his arms up in the air. "You searched me or something?"

"Of course," Bettie said. "There is only so many background checks a woman can do in a Land Rover with bad internet whilst she waits for you to come out,"

Graham just laughed and it was such a cute laugh.

"No you can go and I'm sure I'll see you around," Graham said, extending his hand.

Bettie took his soft warm hand in hers and kissed it. Graham looked excited but in case she never did see this wonderful man, she just wanted one kiss to remember him by.

Bettie got out of the Land Rover but before she shut the door, she just smiled at him.

"I hope to see a lot of you about detective,"

Bettie said.

"Feeling's not mutual," Graham muttered.

Bettie just laughed and really looked forward to seeing this hottie again.

***

15th September 2022
Canterbury, England

"And then she stalked me down in Kent, ran into each other two more times and then we started dating the first time," Graham said.

Bettie just smiled at the beautiful love of her life as he gingerly held her hand in fear of her breaking any more fingers.

Thankfully the hospital bed sheets were wonderfully toasty and warm now that she had been lying here for so long, and as another contraction corkscrewed through her, she just knew that the babies were coming soon.

But the bright lights of the hospital room against the bright white sterile walls were becoming blinding now, and Bettie was seriously looking forward to going home with her new additions to her family and starting her journey as a mother.

That was scary but going to be amazing.

Pure excitement, joy and relief filled her as she stared at her beautiful family round her. Her wonderful nephew and his boyfriend who had loved and supported her through so much, her sister that could be a piece of work but she was amazing in her own way, and the amazing man that had put up with her being a stupid private eye for so long.

She loved them all.

A sharp jab of pain pulsed through her body and

then Bettie just realised. The twins were coming out.

"Graham," Bettie said, through sharp pain. "Be a dear and get the midwife. It's showtime,"

***

15th September 2022
Canterbury, England

A few hours later, Bettie felt completely exhausted as she laid on the hospital bed with the thin blue sheets tightly wrapped around her lower half and she just held the two most amazing babies she had ever seen.

Sean, Harry and Phryne had all left shortly after the birth with Sean and Harry confirming they were definitely gay and never wanted to see a birth again. And Bettie had kicked Phryne out when she commented about Bettie's extreme screaming.

Bettie felt Graham's handsome face resting on her shoulder as they both just looked at the two cutest babies they had made together nine months ago.

The entire room smelt pleasantly of lemons, apples and oranges from an organic solution that the midwife had washed the room down with, and Bettie was just glad to have another smell in the room and it was so amazing to hear the light subtle breathing of her two twins.

At least Bettie's largest fear had been unfounded about the babies being identical, she had always known that they would have a boy and a girl, but she was still scared.

Bettie kissed both the cuties on their little warm heads and both of them smiled at the gesture. They still hadn't been cleaned yet because it was the rules that the babies had to have skin contact with their mothers for at least two hours before anything else was allowed to happen.

And Bettie loved that rule.

"We really have come a long way," Graham said.

Bettie just smiled. "Yep. But a stupid private eye and a idiot cop. We've had some great fights, great cases and great loves,"

Graham kissed her and Bettie loved the feeling of his lips on her.

And then they both went back to looking at their delightful twins in her arms. They really had come so far with each other, now their lives had truly changed forever and there was no going back now.

Bettie knew the next chapter of their lives wouldn't be easy, plain-sailing or completely joyous. There would be challenges. But in Bettie's experience that was exactly the same for all worthwhile things in life.

Bettie had never needed easy, she had only ever needed possible.

And she was really, really looking forward to being a mother and hoping beyond hope that she was going to be an amazing one with her sexy Graham by her side and her sensational family firmly behind her.

And that thought just delighted Bettie more than she ever wanted to admit.

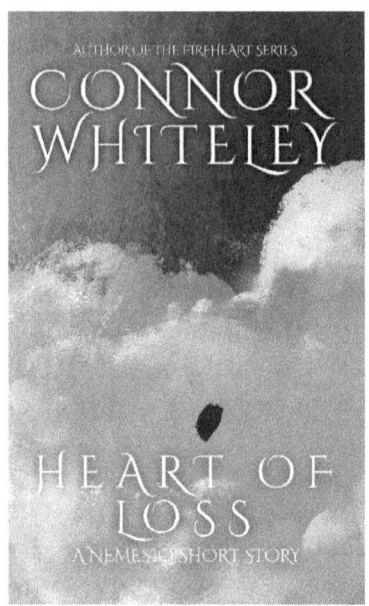

GET YOUR FREE AND EXCLUSIVE SHORT STORY NOW! LEARN ABOUT NEMESIO'S PAST!

https://www.subscribepage.com/fireheart

BETTIE PRIVATE INVESTIGATOR SHORT STORY COLLECTION VOLUME 3

Keep up to date with exclusive deals on Connor Whiteley's Books, as well as the latest news about new releases and so much more!

Sign up for the Grab a Book and Chill Monthly newsletter, and you'll get one **FREE** ebook just for signing up: Agents of The Emperor Collection.

Sign Up Now!

https://dl.bookfunnel.com/f4p5xkprbk

About the author:

Connor Whiteley is the author of over 60 books in the sci-fi fantasy, nonfiction psychology and books for writer's genre and he is a Human Branding Speaker and Consultant.

He is a passionate warhammer 40,000 reader, psychology student and author.

Who narrates his own audiobooks and he hosts The Psychology World Podcast.

All whilst studying Psychology at the University of Kent, England.

Also, he was a former Explorer Scout where he gave a speech to the Maltese President in August 2018 and he attended Prince Charles' 70th Birthday Party at Buckingham Palace in May 2018.

Plus, he is a self-confessed coffee lover!

BETTIE PRIVATE INVESTIGATOR SHORT STORY COLLECTION VOLUME 3

OTHER SHORT STORIES BY CONNOR WHITELEY

<u>Mystery Short Stories:</u>

Protecting The Woman She Hated

Finding A Royal Friend

Our Woman In Paris

Corrupt Driving

A Prime Assassination

Jubilee Thief

Jubilee, Terror, Celebrations

Negative Jubilation

Ghostly Jubilation

Killing For Womenkind

A Snowy Death

Miracle Of Death

A Spy In Rome

The 12:30 To St Pancreas

A Country In Trouble

A Smokey Way To Go

A Spicy Way To GO

A Marketing Way To Go

A Missing Way To Go

A Showering Way To Go

Poison In The Candy Cane

Christmas Innocence

You Better Watch Out

Christmas Theft

Trouble In Christmas
Smell of The Lake
Problem In A Car
Theft, Past and Team
Embezzler In The Room
A Strange Way To Go
A Horrible Way To Go
Ann Awful Way To Go
An Old Way To Go
A Fishy Way To Go
A Pointy Way To Go
A High Way To Go
A Fiery Way To Go
A Glassy Way To Go
A Chocolatey Way To Go
Kendra Detective Mystery Collection Volume 1
Kendra Detective Mystery Collection Volume 2
Stealing A Chance At Freedom
Glassblowing and Death
Theft of Independence
Cookie Thief
Marble Thief
Book Thief
Art Thief
Mated At The Morgue

BETTIE PRIVATE INVESTIGATOR SHORT STORY COLLECTION VOLUME 3

The Big Five Whoopee Moments
Stealing An Election
Mystery Short Story Collection Volume 1
Mystery Short Story Collection Volume 2
Criminal Performance
Candy Detectives
Key To Birth In The Past

Science Fiction Short Stories:
Temptation
Superhuman Autospy
Blood In The Redwater
All Is Dust
Vigil
Emperor Forgive Us
Their Brave New World
Gummy Bear Detective
The Candy Detective
What Candies Fear
The Blurred Image
Shattered Legions
The First Rememberer
Life of A Rememberer
System of Wonder
Lifesaver
Remarkable Way She Died
The Interrogation of Annabella Stormic

Blade of The Emperor
Arbiter's Truth
Computation of Battle
Old One's Wrath
Puppets and Masters
Ship of Plague
Interrogation
Edge of Failure
One Way Choice
Acceptable Losses
Balance of Power
Good Idea At The Time
Escape Plan
Escape In The Hesitation
Inspiration In Need
Singing Warriors
Knowledge is Power
Killer of Polluters
Climate of Death
The Family Mailing Affair
Defining Criminality
The Martian Affair
A Cheating Affair
The Little Café Affair
Mountain of Death
Prisoner's Fight
Claws of Death

BETTIE PRIVATE INVESTIGATOR SHORT STORY COLLECTION VOLUME 3

Bitter Air
Honey Hunt
Blade On A Train
<u>Fantasy Short Stories:</u>
City of Snow
City of Light
City of Vengeance
Dragons, Goats and Kingdom
Smog The Pathetic Dragon
Don't Go In The Shed
The Tomato Saver
The Remarkable Way She Died
The Bloodied Rose
Asmodia's Wrath
Heart of A Killer
Emissary of Blood
Dragon Coins
Dragon Tea
Dragon Rider
Sacrifice of the Soul
Heart of The Flesheater
Heart of The Regent
Heart of The Standing
Feline of The Lost
Heart of The Story
City of Fire
Awaiting Death

Other books by Connor Whiteley:
Bettie English Private Eye Series
A Very Private Woman
The Russian Case
A Very Urgent Matter
A Case Most Personal
Trains, Scots and Private Eyes
The Federation Protects

Lord of War Origin Trilogy:
Not Scared Of The Dark
Madness
Burn Them All

The Fireheart Fantasy Series
Heart of Fire
Heart of Lies
Heart of Prophecy
Heart of Bones
Heart of Fate

City of Assassins (Urban Fantasy)
City of Death
City of Marytrs
City of Pleasure
City of Power

BETTIE PRIVATE INVESTIGATOR SHORT STORY COLLECTION VOLUME 3

<u>Agents of The Emperor</u>
Return of The Ancient Ones
Vigilance
Angels of Fire
Kingmaker
The Eight
The Lost Generation
<u>Lord Of War Trilogy (Agents of The Emperor)</u>
Not Scared Of The Dark
Madness
Burn It All Down

<u>The Garro Series- Fantasy/Sci-fi</u>
GARRO: GALAXY'S END
GARRO: RISE OF THE ORDER
GARRO: END TIMES
GARRO: SHORT STORIES
GARRO: COLLECTION
GARRO: HERESY
GARRO: FAITHLESS
GARRO: DESTROYER OF WORLDS
GARRO: COLLECTIONS BOOK 4-6
GARRO: MISTRESS OF BLOOD
GARRO: BEACON OF HOPE
GARRO: END OF DAYS

Winter Series- Fantasy Trilogy Books
WINTER'S COMING
WINTER'S HUNT
WINTER'S REVENGE
WINTER'S DISSENSION

Miscellaneous:
RETURN
FREEDOM
SALVATION
Reflection of Mount Flame
The Masked One
The Great Deer

Gay Romance Novellas
Breaking, Nursing, Repairing A Broken Heart
Jacob And Daniel
Fallen For A Lie
His Heartstopper
Spying And Weddings

BETTIE PRIVATE INVESTIGATOR SHORT STORY COLLECTION VOLUME 3

All books in 'An Introductory Series':
Careers In Psychology
Psychology of Suicide
Dementia Psychology
Forensic Psychology of Terrorism And Hostage-Taking
Forensic Psychology of False Allegations
Year In Psychology
BIOLOGICAL PSYCHOLOGY 3RD EDITION
COGNITIVE PSYCHOLOGY THIRD EDITION
SOCIAL PSYCHOLOGY- 3RD EDITION
ABNORMAL PSYCHOLOGY 3RD EDITION
PSYCHOLOGY OF RELATIONSHIPS- 3RD EDITION
DEVELOPMENTAL PSYCHOLOGY 3RD EDITION
HEALTH PSYCHOLOGY
RESEARCH IN PSYCHOLOGY
A GUIDE TO MENTAL HEALTH AND TREATMENT AROUND THE WORLD- A GLOBAL LOOK AT DEPRESSION
FORENSIC PSYCHOLOGY
THE FORENSIC PSYCHOLOGY OF THEFT, BURGLARY AND OTHER

CRIMES AGAINST PROPERTY
CRIMINAL PROFILING: A FORENSIC PSYCHOLOGY GUIDE TO FBI PROFILING AND GEOGRAPHICAL AND STATISTICAL PROFILING.
CLINICAL PSYCHOLOGY
FORMULATION IN PSYCHOTHERAPY
PERSONALITY PSYCHOLOGY AND INDIVIDUAL DIFFERENCES
CLINICAL PSYCHOLOGY REFLECTIONS VOLUME 1
CLINICAL PSYCHOLOGY REFLECTIONS VOLUME 2
Clinical Psychology Reflections Volume 3
CULT PSYCHOLOGY
Police Psychology

A Psychology Student's Guide To University
How Does University Work?
A Student's Guide To University And Learning
University Mental Health and Mindset

www.ingramcontent.com/pod-product-compliance
Lightning Source LLC
LaVergne TN
LVHW012119070526
838202LV00056B/5782